One of US

ANNE SCHRAFF

SADDLEBACK
EDUCATIONAL PUBLISHING

URBAN UNDERGROUND

SADDLEBACK
EDUCATIONAL PUBLISHING
www.sdlback.com

© 2010 by Saddleback Educational Publishing

ISBN-13: 978-1-61651-004-6
ISBN-10: 1-61651-004-8
eBook: 978-1-60291-789-7

Printed in Guangzhou, China
0212/CA21200288

16 15 14 13 12 4 5 6 7 8 9

CHAPTER ONE

I really need the job man," Derrick Shaw said to the owner of the 99¢ And More store. The owner called himself Wes, but, in his past and many miles away, he was Waleed. Wes was almost as dark-skinned as Derrick, but he was from Iraq. The store sold everything from food to clothing and cosmetics.

Wes looked the boy over. Derrick was tall and broad shouldered. He probably was never too clever, but he looked honest, though you never could tell. "Kid, what I need is somebody to clean up after we close, straighten up, and something else too. Some customers, they don't come in to buy, if you know what I mean."

Derrick Shaw was struggling to keep a C average at Harriet Tubman High School. He suffered a lot of bullying and abuse because he wasn't sharp, but he managed. "So what do they come in for?" Derrick asked.

"To steal. Shoplifters, you know?" Wes replied.

Derrick frowned. "You'd expect me to stop them?" he asked. Derrick was a peaceful person. In spite of all the humiliation he suffered at the hands of fellow students like Marko Lane, he never struck back. When they mocked his slowness, he tried to laugh along.

"No-no," Wes said, "that's just the thing. I don't want no trouble with the customers, not even the crooks."

Derrick smiled in relief. "That's good, 'cause I don't want any trouble either," he agreed.

"But you got to deal with them, kid. This is what we do," Wes explained. "When they first come in the store, you make eye contact

2

with the customer. You say a friendly 'Hello there and welcome to the store.' Shoplifters don't like contact with the clerks. They don't like to be noticed. So right away, the shoplifter is discouraged. The customer, he smiles back and is happy you are friendly, but the shoplifter, sometimes they're gone right then and there and that's good."

"Yeah," Derrick said. He could do that. He liked people. He had an easy smile. When people took the trouble to get to know Derrick Shaw, they usually liked him. He had a lot of nice friends at Tubman— Jaris Spain, Trevor Jenkins, Alonee Lennox, Sami Archer.

"But sometimes, kid, they will try to steal anyway," Wes went on. "They'll pull some stuff off the shelf. Like, for example, they'll see these T-shirts they like. They look around quick—like, nobody seems to be looking—so they stuff 'em in their purse or bag they got. But you're looking at that big mirror we got in the back of the store and you see what just happened."

"Oh," Derrick said. He was getting worried again. Was he supposed to wrestle the thieves for the stolen merchandise? He didn't think he could do that.

"You wear a big smile, kid, and you go up to this thief and you say in a real friendly voice, 'Hey, we got a sale on shorts that match those T-shirts you got there in your bag. You might want to look at the shorts.' Something like that. So you're not being aggressive. You're just letting them know you seen them take the T-shirts. Nine out of ten times, they'll put the shirts they swiped back before they leave the store. You saved my stuff from being stolen and there's no hassle. You think you could do that, Derrick Shaw?" Wes asked.

Derrick smiled broadly. "Yeah, I could do that, Wes. I can't get into fights with people, but I can sweet-talk 'em into doing the right thing," he said. "I hate trouble."

"Me too," Wes agreed. "I don't want no trouble with people, even bad people." Wes was a short, round man. He was forty-three years old and he'd immigrated to the United States ten years earlier with his wife and four children. "Okay then, Derrick," Wes continued, "I can only pay minimum wage. If that's okay, you come here after school tomorrow—we'll work out which days then—and you work until we close, usually around nine. On Saturday I'll need you all day, but we close on Sunday. How does that sound to you?"

"Sounds great, Wes," Derrick responded. "Like I said, I need a job bad. We got five kids in our family. My pop, he's a good carpenter, but they ain't building as many houses as they used to, and he's lucky if he works a coupla days a week. I'm the oldest kid. Mom was really hoping I could bring in some money to help out with the rent and stuff. So could I start tomorrow?"

"I'll look for you tomorrow, Derrick," Wes nodded. "After school."

"I ride my bike to school and I could ride it here too," Derrick thought out loud. "Thanks a lot, Wes! It'll be great to go home and tell Mom and Pop I got a job. Man you really made my day, Wes. You won't be sorry either. I'm a good worker. I can stock the shelves and mop the floors, and I'll keep an eye on that big mirror in the back and do my best there too."

"Great," Wes said.

"I like people," Derrick added. "I've always liked people. I can deal with them. I've had paper routes and all my customers liked me. They really did."

Derrick left the store and jumped on his bike. Derrick was a fast biker. He could get home from the store in about fifteen minutes.

The Shaw family lived in an apartment on Choctaw Street. There were apartments up and down the street, not in excellent repair, but not run-down either. Most of the tenants were hardworking people who tried to keep their places clean. When somebody dumped an old mattress or sofa in the alleys, the men would get together and drag it away. They didn't want this to be like some areas across Grant where kids grew up amid mountains of trash and rats scurried around their places.

"Mom, Pop!" Derrick shouted as he came into the apartment. "I got a job at that ninety-nine-cent store. Real nice guy hired me. His name is Wes. I'm starting tomorrow."

Mom came to give Derrick a big hug. Pop stood behind her, smiling. "I knew you'd get work, boy. You got the touch," Pop beamed.

The other kids in the family gathered around Derrick. Bruce was fourteen, Kayla was twelve, Juno was ten, and little Talia was six. "I like that store," Kayla said. "You can get nice bracelets and stuff real cheap."

"Now, we're not goin' to be spending money on foolish geegaws," Mom chided. "You know your daddy ain't been working steady, and Derrick's money gonna help pay the rent and the gas and electric."

Derrick's father was a burly, good-natured man who earned good money while the building boom was going on.

"Now Florida," he said to his wife. "It ain't gonna bust us for the kids to spend a little extra. We ain't goin' to be without electric lights if Kayla buys a hair ribbon or Juno gets a bag of bubblegum. I'm still working. I'm bringin' in money and things are gonna be lookin' up real soon."

Florida Shaw looked at her husband. She loved Guthrie Shaw as much as the day she married him, when she was eighteen and he was twenty. She'd just graduated from Tubman High, and Guthrie had finished the two-year course at a community college that made him a carpenter.

"I'd like to get me a job too," Bruce chimed in. "Lotta things I can do."

Derrick grinned at his little brother. "You're just fourteen, boy," Derrick told him. "You gotta do good in middle school. You're smarter than me, Bruce. You gonna be the brains in the family that gets to go to college."

"You can go to the community college too, Derrick," Mom assured him. "You can do that."

CHAPTER ONE

"No Mom, I'm too dumb," Derrick protested. "I got one more year after this one at Tubman and then I'm done."

"You are letting those no-good boys at Tubman cut you down, baby," Mom insisted indignantly. "Don't you pay no never-mind to trash-talking boys like Marko Lane who try to make their own selves better than they are by cutting down other people."

Derrick smiled at his mother. He knew she loved him and thought highly of him. But deep in Derrick's heart he feared he just didn't have what it took to rise much above minimum wage jobs.

The next day at school, Derrick could think of little else but his job. He'd be making more money than he'd ever made on his other jobs. He had run paper routes, picked fruit, and done yard work. But this was a real job, and Wes seemed like a good guy. It would be nice working in the store and getting to meet the customers. Derrick even enjoyed the thought of the challenge: Could he prevent shoplifting without getting anybody mad? Derrick thought of himself as sort of a friendly peace officer, stopping crime without getting rough on anybody.

After his last class at Tubman, Derrick jumped on his bike. He'd told all his friends about his great new job. Jaris Spain, who was much smarter than Derrick, had a really crummy job at the Chicken Shack. "I'm dishing out this greasy food all night," Jaris complained, "and you'll be working in a real store, dude. Way to go!" Jaris clapped Derrick on the back and high-fived him.

Derrick was on top of his world as he rode off to work.

"Hey kid," Wes shouted when Derrick biked up to the shop. "You're ten minutes early. I like that!"

Derrick hurried inside and began straightening up the merchandise and sweeping the floor. He had been working for about an hour when two girls from Tubman High came in. He recognized them. Ryann and Leticia were not friends of Derrick's, but he always said 'Hi' to them at school. Two freshmen from

Tubman, whom Derrick didn't know, were with them. The four girls hurried down to the T-shirt racks.

Derrick smiled at the girls and greeted them, but Ryann made a face and whispered something to Leticia. Derrick thought they were making fun of him. A lot of kids did. Or else maybe they were thinking about shoplifting and they resented Derrick greeting them.

Derrick continued to straighten the shelves, but he kept his eye on the big mirror at the back of the store. He saw Ryann and Leticia stuffing lipsticks into their purses. Derrick's heart sank. Here it was already—a problem. And he had to deal with it. He didn't expect he'd be tested so soon. But he had to act.

Derrick sauntered down to the cosmetics aisle, a big smile on his face. "You know what, girls?" he said. "I got a little sister— Kayla—and she's wearing lipstick already. Mom's really mad that she's wearing lipstick when she's only twelve. But, you know, she

11

tried that lipstick you just took and it dried her lips so bad . . . it's not the best kind, you know. Why don't you go over to the next aisle? The lipstick there is just as cheap and it's good—doesn't dry your lips . . . "

Ryann gasped. Leticia looked frightened.

"Ohhh," Ryann exclaimed with fake shock. "Did we put lipstick in our purses?"

"Oh, people do that all the time," Derrick replied, still smiling. "They get so busy picking stuff out that they just forget to go to the cash register . . . "

Ryann smiled. "You're nice, Derrick. I see you in class all the time. You're really nice. Here, put these lipsticks back for us, okay?"

"Sure Ryann," Derrick said. "I can do that."

Derrick heard Leticia say as they walked away, "I always thought he was some big idiot, but he's really cool. He's sweet."

Derrick hadn't seen Wes lurking behind the makeup display, watching the whole scene unfold. After the girls paid for two lipsticks that they picked out on the other aisle and left the store, Wes appeared. He grabbed Derrick's hand and shook it. "You're a natural!" he said. "I couldn't have handled that better myself. I'm so glad you came here looking for work, kid!"

The afternoon and early evening flew by. Derrick was busy all the time, but he was enjoying himself. The only downside was that he'd have a couple hours of homework when he got home, around nine-thirty. But that was okay.

After he finished working, Derrick hopped on his bike for the ride home. It was dark now and the crescent moon hung in the sky like a cardboard cutout. Derrick wasn't good at science, but he enjoyed looking at the night sky and finding the planets and the Big Dipper.

Derrick knew all the shortcuts, and he pedaled through an alley that would cut off about five minutes from his trip home. But then, as Derrick was halfway down the alley, he heard a gunshot—a sharp crack and a flash—just a few yards from where he was. Derrick skidded to a stop and jumped off his bike, preparing to run for cover. But before he could move, he saw a body that had been hurled against a garbage pail by the impact of the gunfire. He felt as though he was caught in a horror movie, but this was happening in real time. The body—a man's body—quivered for a moment before the head dropped back grotesquely against the garbage pail.

"Oh my God! Oh my God!" Derrick gasped. The blood seemed to run from his arms and legs. He was numb. He wanted to get away from here as fast as he could, but the shooter confronted him. "Don't make a move dude," he warned.

Derrick stared at the short kid with the gun in his hand. *He knew him*. His name was B.J. Brady and he went to Tubman High School when he was a freshman. Then he dropped out. Everyone in the neighborhood knew he was now a drug dealer. "B.J.," Derrick groaned.

"He's one of us," Derrick thought with horror. "He just killed a man and he's *one of us* . . ."

"Hey," B.J. went on, "I remember you. You're the big dumb guy everybody hassled. You're Derrick . . ."

"Please, B.J.," Derrick rasped hoarsely, "don't shoot me, please."

"I got to," B.J. said. "You just saw what happened."

"No!" Derrick insisted. "That guy there . . . we got to get help for him. Call nine-one-one. You got a cell? He'll be okay . . . please, get help for him."

B.J. laughed a harsh laugh without any warmth in it. "You freakin' fool, he's dead. Can't you see that? He's dead, you big fool."

"No!" Derrick gasped. "Maybe they can save him." Derrick didn't know the young man on the ground, and he barely remembered B.J.

"I'm tellin' you, fool, he's dead. Don't you know what that means?" B.J. chided.

"And you saw me do it. I gotta off you too man. I don't want to but I gotta."

Derrick felt like he was choking. He couldn't take a deep breath. His chest was getting tight, and the few lights in the alley coming from the apartment windows blurred. "No, please B.J.! I'm helping my family. We got five kids and my pop isn't working a lot. I'm the oldest. I just got a job. I just started today. It's gonna be a big help to my family. Don't kill me, B.J. I swear I won't tell anybody what I saw. I swear I won't."

Even though Derrick wasn't very smart, he knew how stupid it was to expect a break from a guy who just killed someone in cold blood. Why would somebody like B.J. care if a guy was helping his distressed family? B.J. just shot a man to death in the alley with no more hesitation than if his victim had been a rat.

Then Derrick remembered. He hadn't thought about it in years. Something had happened when he was eight years old and B.J. was ten. Derrick was hanging with Jaris and Trevor, and they were skateboarding. They were falling down more than they were riding. Along comes this ten-year-old, about their size because he was small for his age. He was a fifth grader and they were third graders, but they all bonded.

"Hey suckas," B.J. yelled. "You doin' it all wrong. Lemme show you how it's done dudes."

That day and in the weeks that followed, he taught them how to ride those skateboards over curbs, how to fly through the air, and how to land as smoothly as professionals. They were friends—Jaris, Trevor, Derrick, and B.J.—riding the boards.

"Hey B.J.," Derrick reminded B.J. "Remember when you taught us how to ride our skateboards? I remember the first time I flipped the board and landed upright because of what you told me to do.

Remember how you got us all jumping off curbs and flying?" Derrick's mouth was dry and he was shaking.

"So what?" B.J. sneered. "Thing is dude, you come down the wrong alley at the wrong time. You can't be out there breathing after that. You can tell the cops what you saw and I'm facing murder one, y'hear what I'm saying? So how you want it—in the front or in the back?"

"B.J., we were brothers . . . we were a team . . . please don't do this," Derrick was nearly crying. "We were family B.J. You were one of us."

"I got no family," B.J. snarled. "Never had one. My parents turned on me. Listen dude, I gotta git. Why don't you make it easy on yourself and turn around so you don't see it coming . . ."

"I swear I'll never tell anybody about what I saw B.J.," Derrick pleaded. "I'll forget about it. I'll never tell a soul. I swear to you. I'll never tell anybody . . . please B.J., don't shoot me. I'm beggin' you.

I never did anything wrong to you, B.J. I won't rat you out . . . not never."

B.J. stood there staring at Derrick. The hand holding the gun seemed to waver a little, as though B.J. was considering changing his plans. Hope leaped in Derrick's breast. Derrick didn't go to church with his mother as often as she wanted him to, but now his lips moved silently in frantic pleas: "Save me, please save me."

"Dude, if I don't shoot you and you go back on your word, *I'll get you,*" B.J. warned. "You know that, don't you? I'll get your family too. Y'hear what I'm telling you? You rat me out and even if I'm dead, I'll get you somehow. You rat me out and nobody in your family will ever be able to close their eyes in sleep without thinking there's going to be a guy at the window with a gun." Then he lowered the gun. "Get on that bike and get out of here, fool. And don't look back. Don't ever look back."

CHAPTER TWO

Derrick was shaking so badly he could hardly get on his bike. When he was in the seat, he almost toppled over, but somehow he got it moving. He was drenched in perspiration even though it was a chilly night. He needed to get out of here fast. He couldn't believe that B.J. had actually spared him. As he pedaled from the alley, he expected at any moment that a bullet would rip into his spine and it would all be over.

As he biked away, Derrick glanced at the man with his head against the garbage pail. He was young. A horrible thought came to Derrick. Maybe he was still alive! Maybe he was just unconscious, and, if the

20

doctors got to him, they could save him. Derrick didn't know where B.J. was. Maybe he was still lurking in the darkness, watching Derrick. If Derrick stopped for a closer look at the dead man, maybe that would be B.J.'s reason to shoot him after all.

Derrick had to keep going out of the alley. He sped up to the main street, where many stores were open. He stopped the bike and looked around. There was no sign of B.J.

Most of the juniors at Tubman High School had cell phones, but not Derrick. His parents couldn't afford to let him have one. So Derrick found one of the few pay phones still operating outside a drugstore. He looked around again to make sure B.J. wasn't there. The street was empty except for an old couple walking their dog.

Derrick went in the pay phone booth and dialed 9-1-1. When the dispatcher came on, he blurted, "In the alley off Grant, behind the VFW Thrift Store . . . a dead guy. I think he's dead." Then Derrick hung up. He had done his duty. If by some remote chance the guy was still alive, help was on the way. Derrick could not have lived with himself if he hadn't at least made the call for the guy.

Derrick got back on his bike and pedaled for home. The dead guy's face was imprinted on his brain. He had a terrible head wound, but his face was intact except for a rivulet of blood alongside his nose.

Derrick pedaled faster. He was amazed that his legs could pump so fast. His mind was spinning crazily. He wanted this to be a dream, a nightmare. He wanted to wake up in bed and be grateful that it had only been a dream. He wanted it to go away.

Derrick began planning his story then. He would tell his parents everything had gone well at work but he was very tired. He wasn't used to being on his feet like that. All he needed was a good night's rest and he'd be fine.

"Hi Darlin'," Mom greeted Derrick when he came in. "How'd it go baby?"

"Great Mom. Wes, my boss, he likes me. Real good," Derrick replied. "I'm just a little tired. I'm goin' to bed."

"You look funny, son," Pop remarked. "You sure you're all right?" Pop looked concerned.

Mom came to Derrick and ran the palm of her hand down his wet cheek. "Lordy, you are all sweaty, baby. You ain't comin' down with a fever are you?" she asked.

"No Mom. I biked real fast coming home. I got to sweating. And another thing, I had this burrito with hot sauce and it sorta upset my stomach. But I'm fine. Everything is great, Mom. I'm gonna shower and then I'm going to bed. I'll do my homework tomorrow . . . I haven't got that much."

"You get your rest, baby," Mom told him.

Derrick got into the shower and let the hot water pour over his hair and his body. Strangely, he thought the hot water could wash away what happened to him tonight, with all its fear and horror. He remembered seeing a very old movie once, starring an actor named Kirk Douglas. In the movie Douglas talked about pulling his brain from his head and rinsing away the terrible thoughts that were tormenting him. That's what Derrick wanted to do, but he couldn't.

When Derrick got into bed, all he could see in his mind's eye was the dead man's head against the metal garbage pail. B.J. had shot him in the head. But you could tell he'd been a handsome young man.

Derrick had never seen that face before. He wasn't a student at Tubman High. He looked about twenty. Derrick wondered who he was. Were his parents sitting somewhere watching the hands of the clock and wondering why their son wasn't coming home? Or did he live by himself, so his parents didn't even know he wasn't coming home tonight and would never come home again?

Derrick also wondered why B.J. shot him? What had he done? What would give B.J. reason enough to kill a man like that?

Then the amazing fact came to Derrick: B.J. had spared his life. Even though Derrick saw what had happened and could destroy B.J., the shooter had spared him. How could he have done that? How could someone kill like that and yet spare Derrick.

Derrick tossed and turned all night. He closed his eyes but sleep was impossible, even for a few minutes.

In the morning, when Derrick came to the breakfast table, the television was on. He heard fragments of the news story. He heard his father saying, "What a terrible shame. A nineteen-year-old boy dying right in our neighborhood, shot down in an alley. What's this world coming to?"

The younger children were still in bed, but fourteen-year-old Bruce was looking at the television. "Look, there's his picture. I never seen him around here. Did you, Derrick?" Bruce asked.

Derrick snatched a quick look at the screen. A bolt of horror ran through him. He had seen that face last night all right.

He'd never forget it. Not as long as he lived. "Doesn't look familiar, Bruce," Derrick replied. "Not from around here . . ."

As the younger children started coming to breakfast, Mom shut off the TV. She didn't want them seeing the news and getting scared.

"Said his name was Rafe Wexford," Pop commented. "I never heard of no family around here with that name. Maybe he was just passing through."

Kayla sat down at the breakfast table. She looked at Derrick and asked, "Did you have fun at your job, Derrick?" She had big, bright eyes and her hair was done in many braids. Derrick thought she was a beautiful little girl. Looking at her always brought Derrick joy. But now he felt another emotion, a horrible and unwanted emotion—fear. Derrick looked at his little sister and he heard B.J.'s threatening voice, cold and hard and deadly, "*I'll get your family too.*"

Derrick forced the threat from his mind and smiled at Kayla. "Yeah, my job went real good. Some teenaged girls were stealing stuff and I got them to put it back. Then I told them about what you said about that nice lipstick," he told her.

"*You did?*" Kayla exclaimed, grinning broadly.

"Yeah, I said my sister swears by this lipstick and they oughta really buy some 'cause my sister is smart,'" Derrick told her.

"Wow," Kayla said, "did they buy some?"

"Yep," Derrick said. "You bet they did."

"You are too young to be wearing lipstick, girl," Pop grunted. "You are just a baby."

"I am *not* a baby," Kayla insisted, tossing her braids in annoyance. "I'm in middle school. *Everybody* in middle school wears makeup."

"Not everybody," Pop countered, "and I don't care if they do. You shouldn't be doing it."

For a little while, being with his family blocked out the horrible ordeal Derrick went through last night. But as Derrick got ready for school, the nightmare came back to him. He dreaded what would surely be the main topic of conversation this morning at Tubman. Everybody would have something to say about it, and Derrick would have to be very careful not to reveal any knowledge about what happened in the alley.

As Derrick rolled into Tubman on his bike and locked it into the rack next to the parking lot, Trevor and Jaris came along. "Hey Derrick," Trevor called, "did you hear about the guy getting offed in the alley behind the thrift store last night?"

"Yeah," Derrick answered. "It was on TV this morning."

"Man," Jaris went on, "my parents are all freaked about it. They want to pick me up now when I work late at the Chicken Shack. I hate that. I told them it had to be some gang stuff. It wasn't a random killing."

"I never heard of the guy," Trevor chimed in. "Rafe Wexford. They said he was a college student at City. I never heard that name before in this neighborhood. Nobody recognized his picture from the TV either."

"Derrick, you work over at the ninety-nine-cent store now," Jaris noted. "Isn't that sort of on your way home? Man, they said the killing happened after nine. You're lucky you weren't coming through around then. I bet just thinking about that gives you the creeps."

"Yeah," Derrick agreed. "You never know what's right around the corner . . ."

"You better be careful riding that bike home at night down those mean streets," Sami Archer commanded Derrick. "I wonder who that boy was? Somebody's child, no matter what kind of trouble he was in. That's what my mama always says when she sees a homeless person or a sad case. 'That's some mother's child,' she goes."

Derrick was shaking inside as he headed for English. B.J. would probably be caught, Derrick figured—B.J. was probably connected in some way to the dead man. Derrick was scared stiff that B.J. would think he had gone to the police even though he didn't. Derrick tried to convince himself that B.J. had to know you can't get away with murder. Sure, unlike Derrick, B.J. was clever. Sure, he'd gotten himself out of many tight spots. But B.J. had to know you can't shoot a man down in the street like that and go free forever.

Mr. Pippin had not yet arrived in his English class, so everybody was talking about the murder. "Wasn't no drive-by shooting," Marko Lane insisted. "Cops aren't saying much, but the buzz is that it was like execution-style. No fight starting at a party and ending up in the alley. This dude was fingered. My cousin lives over there. He says there was just one shot. Everybody thought it was a firecracker. No car screeching away. Murderer musta escaped on foot. Maybe had a friend waiting nearby."

"They brought him into the hospital where my mom works in the ER," a girl added. "He was gone before they even wheeled him in. Dead on arrival. The killer made that first shot count."

Derrick wanted to clamp his hands over his ears. If only they'd stop talking about it. He couldn't stand it.

"Hey look at dopey there," Marko laughed. "He looks real upset. What's the matter, Derrick? You scared the bad guy who wasted that Wexford dude is after you?"

"I'm just trying to finish this story we're gonna talk about in class," Derrick mumbled.

"Naw, he's scared," Marko pressed. "Poor baby. You want somebody should go get a teddy bear you can hold?"

"Knock it off, freak," Kevin Walker hissed from his desk.

"Watch who you're callin' a freak man," Marko shot back. "We don't need no weirdo from a cow farm in Texas telling us what we can talk about."

Mr. Pippin came in then and there was quiet. Ever since Marko Lane and his friends had been punished with detention for disrupting this class, Mr. Pippin had gained a little control. But Marko didn't intend to let go of his mocking of Derrick

31

entirely. "Mr. Pippin, sir," Marko said with mock respect. "I think Derrick there needs a glass of water. He's really scared 'cause of that murder last night. He's sweatin' like crazy, Mr. Pippin."

Mr. Pippin glared at Marko. Then he turned to Derrick. "Are you all right, Derrick?" he asked.

"Yes sir, I'm fine," Derrick replied.

"Good," Mr. Pippin said, glaring again at Marko.

After class, as the students were filing out, Marko stabbed his finger into Derrick's spine and yelled, "It's a gun, Derrick!"

Derrick jumped in fright and Marko exploded in laughter. "Don't do stuff like that, Marko," Derrick moaned with anguish on his face.

Jaris came alongside Marko and suggested, "Why don't you jump in the john and flush yourself?"

"Nobody got a sense of humor anymore?" Marko laughed.

"Not when it comes to dead guys lying in alleys, Marko," Alonee told him with disgust. "We're all kind of on edge. Somebody murdered not far from here. That's a horrible thing. I just talked to my mom on my cell and she says they're saying he graduated from Lincoln and he was a good pole vaulter at City too."

"Yeah," Kevin recalled, "when we had that meet against Lincoln, I think I saw him. He was cheering his old friends on."

Derrick escaped from the group of students while they kept talking about the murder. He couldn't listen to anymore of it. He knew what his duty was. Fear or no fear, he should be going to the police. He should be telling them he saw B.J. Brady murder Wexford. Any decent citizen would do that. How many times had Derrick heard his own parents express rage and disappointment because fear kept many people in the neighborhood from cooperating with the police after terrible crimes?

"They're nothin' but low cowards," Mom had called them when a murder last year went unsolved. "People out there know what happened. They know who done it. But they're afraid to speak up."

"They won't say nothin'," Pop joined in. "They won't stand up and do their duty. If everybody gonna be scared of their own shadow, that's like giving the killers a free pass. They can roam around and take folks down like it's hunting season on people."

Derrick felt sick and guilty, but he didn't know what to do. In exchange for his life, Derrick had given B.J. his promise that he wouldn't tell anybody. It came down to that. B.J. was at the point of asking Derrick if he wanted to be shot from the front or the back. Derrick was that close to dying. And B.J. spared him.

B.J. let Derrick live and for that Derrick promised silence. He swore silence. He couldn't go back on his word. He was afraid to go back on it. B.J. could have killed Derrick in that alley. From his standpoint, it would have been the smart thing to do. That meant something, didn't it? That had to mean something. Derrick didn't understand how B.J. could spare him only moments after taking the life of another man. Derrick didn't feel smart enough to solve such a mystery.

That evening, the local television news was full of the murder story. But there was a heartbreaking new twist. Rafe's father had been an officer in the war in Iraq. He was a much decorated soldier who lost his life when a roadside bomb near Baghdad exploded. That made Rafe's mother a war widow with one son—Rafe.

There were clips of Rafe as a pole vaulter at Lincoln High and City College. There were scenes of his high school graduation. Most tragic of all, there was footage of his father's funeral with full military honors. The sobbing widow held the folded flag from her husband's coffin while the teenaged boy at her side, Rafe, held her arm. Now there would be nobody to hold her arm.

Derrick was grief stricken to see the coverage. Derrick felt he owed that weeping mother the truth about how her son died. She deserved—what did they call it?—closure. She wanted to know who killed her baby. She wanted that person brought to justice. It was only right. She deserved to know. B.J. deserved to pay for his crime.

But Derrick's own words were seared into his mind.

"I swear I'll never tell anybody about what I saw B.J. I'll forget about it. I'll never tell a soul. I swear to you."

Derrick sat on the grass with his lunch, but he couldn't get the bologna sandwich down. It was dressed with mustard and relish, but he couldn't swallow it. He hung his head and felt the entire world was on his shoulders.

"Hi Derrick," Destini Fletcher, another junior, was standing there. "I got nobody to eat lunch with. Can I sit here with you?"

"Sure Destini," Derrick answered. She was a pretty girl. Ordinarily, Derrick would have been thrilled to have her want to join him for lunch. Girls weren't generally crazy about Derrick. Derrick remembered that, some time back, Destini was in a relationship with a guy who ended up hitting her. He felt sorry for her to have gone through that.

"Don't you like your sandwich, Derrick?" Destini asked. "I'll give you half of mine. I've got an egg salad sandwich."

"My sandwich is good," Derrick replied. "Mom makes good sandwiches. I'm just not real hungry."

"Trouble at home?" Destini asked.

"No. I guess it's that murder," Derrick said softly. "That's so sad. I hate when people do violent things, Destini. I don't even like violent movies. I can't stand them even if they're supposed to be funny. All the guys think I'm weird because they like these movies where a dozen guys are getting killed, but I hate them. I must be some kind of a freak or something."

"No," Destini asserted, "they're the freaks. Just because there's more of them than us doesn't mean they're right and we're wrong. Tyron took me to this gross movie where some madman was cutting people up with a chain saw. He and the other guys were laughing their heads off, but it was sick. I sort of liked this guy, I guess 'cause he seemed to like me. But then I figured it out. He had this violence in him. He liked to see people suffering in the movie. And he ended up hurting me too. It's all part of the same thing, Derrick. So don't be ashamed that you're a gentle person." Destini smiled and patted Derrick on the shoulder. "Just think of it like this, Derrick. If there were more people like you in the world, there wouldn't be so many wars, and millions and millions of people wouldn't have to die."

Derrick smiled at the girl. He liked her.

CHAPTER THREE

Derrick decided he would never again take the shortcut through the alley where he'd seen the terrible event. He would keep to the main street no matter how much longer it took him to get home. Of course, avoiding that spot would not make him any safer. B.J. never stayed in one place. B.J. was all over the neighborhood. His main hangout was Papa's Pool Hall, a dive off Grant Avenue. Derrick had seen him several times spending time there, dressed in fancy silk shirts with gold chains around his neck. Everybody knew he was dealing drugs, but the few times he was arrested he always slithered out of the rap. Derrick thought if he ever saw B.J. again, just the sight of him would give Derrick a heart attack. Just seeing that face and knowing what he did would be too much to bear.

"Hey kid," Wes called out as Derrick came to work. "Good to see you."

"Hi," Derrick said, eager to work. He needed something to distract him. He was glad to be at the busy store, where there was always something to do—cleaning up, arranging the merchandise, helping customers, and keeping an eye out for shoplifters. Little kids often came by after school to rip off candy. Stealing some candy was no big deal for a kid, but like Wes said, "It's step number one for them. You take little things when you're little. Then you get bigger and you take big things, like cars."

Derrick's mother, with Juno and Talia in tow, stopped in about an hour after Derrick came to work. Derrick smiled at his little brother and sister and showed them where the best deals on toys were. If you selected the right bag, you could end up with twenty-four spacemen and aliens for the same price you paid for another bag with only twelve action figures. "Look here, Juno," Derrick advised. "You can fill up your whole space ship with this stuff."

"Yeah!" Juno cried, "and they got swords and death ray guns and everything. David's spacemen aren't as good. My spacemen win every time when we fight."

Derrick went over to help Talia pick out sprinkly hair ribbons. He heard his mother thanking Wes for hiring her son. "He speaks very highly of you," Mom told Wes.

"He's a great kid," Wes answered. "I've had lots of kids working here and he's the best I ever had. He's a winner."

Mom came over to where Derrick was working and said, "Did you hear what Wes said about you, baby? Didn't I always tell you how wonderful you were, and not to listen to those fools who were trying to pull you down? Wes is a businessman who knows what he's talking about."

As Derrick worked, he glanced at the local newspaper on the stand. There was a picture of Rafe Wexford on the front page. Derrick turned away and busied himself by straightening out the magazines. Maybe Derrick wouldn't have felt so badly if Rafe had turned out to be a gangbanger with a long police record. It wouldn't have made it okay for B.J. to shoot him, but it would have made it easier for Derrick. But Rafe seemed to be a straight-arrow guy, an athlete and a scholar, the son of a war hero. There seemed to be no reason for him to have been in B.J.'s murderous path. Why would B.J. take the life of a good young man and then turn around to spare another person's life?

"So this is where you work, eh Derrick?" Marko Lane remarked, swinging into the 99¢ store with Jasmine and several other kids from Tubman who hung with him.

"Yeah, this is where I work," Derrick said. "Can I help you guys find anything?"

Marko took a can of spaghetti and meatballs off the shelf and asked, "Is this good stuff? It's a lot cheaper than in the supermarket. Maybe it's really dog food with a label that says spaghetti and meatballs. What do you say dude? Are they pulling a scam on us?"

Jasmine and the other kids nearly fell over laughing. Marko looked at them with appreciation. He always enjoyed giving them a laugh.

"I bet you wouldn't know the difference if somebody served you dog food and said it was spaghetti and meatballs," Marko said to Derrick.

"This is good stuff," Derrick explained calmly. "It's the exact same stuff you get in the supermarket. See, what happens is, they make too much of something and then they sell a bunch of it to these ninety-nine-cent stores and they sell them cheaper, but it's the same stuff. Last year you would've paid three times more for this can."

Marko nudged Jasmine. "Hear what the dude is sayin', babe. This stuff is *old*. This food is ten years old and it's gone rotten and now we get to buy it cheap," Marko crowed, arousing another spasm of hysterical laughter from his group.

"No," Derrick replied cheerfully, using the information Wes had given him when he started here. "See, on the bottom of the can it says 'Best by' a date. The date here is two years from now, so the food is good until then and even later on. So you're good to go buying this spaghetti and meatballs."

"Hey, the dude can read," Marko pretended surprise. "I didn't think you could read, Derrick."

Jasmine giggled. "Oh come on Marko. I see Derrick reading all the time. He reads *Baby Bear Goes to the Market* and *How Raccoon Found a Friend.*

Derrick looked at Jasmine. He wondered if she was a nice person at one time. Had her friendship with Marko made her cruel and sarcastic? Or was she drawn to somebody like Marko because she was already that kind of person? Derrick had a strange question. Who knows what people are really like? Are they what their friends say they are? Are they what their parents or their teachers say they are?

Derrick wondered what people would say about him? He knew his parents would say nice things because they loved him. His parents were proud of him, even though they knew he was often bullied and mocked. Derrick knew his friends liked him. But who was he really?

Who was Rafe Wexford really? Everybody described him as a nice young man. What was there about him that made B.J. Brady kill him?

While these thoughts flashed through Derrick's mind, Jasmine continued reciting Derrick's alleged library of books. "And I *saw* him reading *How Baby Bird Learned to Fly*.

Derrick felt hurt, but he didn't hate Jasmine. He didn't hate Marko either. One day Kevin Walker and Derrick were studying together, and Marko came over and started making ugly taunts. Kevin turned to

Derrick and told him, "Sometimes I'd just love to smash his face in so hard his nose'd come out the back of his head." Kevin had a fierce temper, but Derrick didn't. He couldn't even hate the people making fun of him. Derrick might feel hurt, but he always thought the persons mocking him must deep down be sad and miserable or they wouldn't find pleasure in hurting others.

When Jasmine came down the aisle where Derrick was working, he turned to her and remarked, "Jasmine, I feel so sorry for you."

The smile left Jasmine's face. "What are you talking about?" she demanded. She looked a little alarmed. "Why should *you* feel sorry for *me*?"

"Because, Jasmine," Derrick explained, "you got so much going for you. You're pretty and you're smart. You got a nice family. But here you are wasting your time making fun of a dodo like me. There must be a lot of sad stuff in your heart to make you wanna do that."

Jasmine stared at Derrick. "I was . . . just . . . joking," she stammered.

"No Jasmine," Derrick corrected her. "You were making fun of me. It's okay. I'm not mad. I just feel bad for you."

Jasmine's gleeful smile—the one she wore all the while Marko was making fun of Derrick and while she was reciting the titles of the books she said he read—did not return. "Let's look at lipstick," she said to Marko.

"Hey Derrick," Marko said to him, "good thing the guy who owns this store didn't give you an IQ test before he hired you 'cause—"

"Marko!" Jasmine snapped. "Would you come over here and help me pick out a nice shade of lipstick? Tell me which shade of pink you like. Stop making childish comments over there and make yourself useful."

Marko went over to help Jasmine.

After work that night, Derrick was nervous riding home, even though he traveled the main, well lighted streets. Sometimes he'd bike through a place without much light, and the shadows seemed to crowd around him, like living things.

Derrick had a lot of studying to do for American history and English. He thought he could finish his junior year with maybe a C plus if he was lucky. But all the time he was studying, he was thinking about B.J. Brady.

Derrick thought back again to the time when they were all kids playing on the streets named for Native American tribes. B.J.'s ten-year-old peers called him a "stupid runt" but he fit in well with the eight-year-olds, Jaris, Derrick, Trevor. B.J. was part of that younger gang, though the fact that he played with eight-year-olds was fodder for the kids who made fun of him. "You playin' with babies fool," they'd jeer at him as he jumped on his skateboard with Derrick and Jaris. Even some of the eight-year-olds, like Marko, mocked him. "Hey sucka," Marko would yell, "how come you so old and playin' with us?"

They were on their skateboards all summer—flying, crashing, unafraid of the bruised shins and split lips. Derrick remembered those really good times, and B.J. was the reason for a lot of them. Because he was older and more cunning than the rest, he knew ways to bend the rules and increase the fun. He could get them all into the movies for free, by sneaking in an unlocked back door. He'd steal fruit and even apple pies cooling on window sills, and they would all feast, untroubled by conscience.

But then, while they were still in middle school, B.J. went on to Tubman and he was soon failing. His friends didn't hang with him anymore. B.J. was into drugs even then. In ninth grade, attending school got too intense for B.J. From time to time the old gang ran into him—sometimes Derrick, sometimes Jaris or Trevor—but it wasn't the same anymore. He now lived in a different world. "How did it come to this?" Derrick wondered, as he tried desperately to concentrate on the story for English.

Bruce came into the room while Derrick was studying. His little brother was making really good grades in school. He was especially good in math. But Mom and Pop took pains not to compare him with Derrick at that age. They were good like that.

"Hey Derrick, anybody at your school know that dead guy? I bet they were talking about him, huh?" Bruce asked.

"Nobody knew him," Derrick replied.

"They're gonna bury him next week," Bruce went on. "It said on TV that the people around the alley where the cops found him have put up a memorial, flowers and stuff, you know, American flags. You know how they do when a kid gets killed in an accident? Pop says somebody out there knows who did it. I'd tell the cops if I knew. I wouldn't let no freakin' murderer get away with doing that."

Derrick began to sweat. The conversation was getting too painful. "People get scared, Bruce. Remember when that lady reported on some gangbangers who killed a guy?

They firebombed her house and she died, and then her kids didn't have anybody. People think about stuff like that and they don't want to talk, you know?" he explained.

"But if nobody says anything, then the killer is gonna get away and he'll kill somebody else," Bruce said.

"Yeah," Derrick agreed sadly. Derrick returned his attention to his English textbook and Bruce got the message and wandered away. Derrick wondered if he was the only witness. Maybe somebody else saw something too. Maybe some old lady was sitting at the window with her cat looking out on the alley, and maybe she saw everything. She'd probably tell the police everything she knew because she was old and didn't have anybody and she wouldn't care what happened to her.

But Derrick had his family to worry about.

Derrick remembered other murders in the neighborhood. There had been five in the past six years, and only one was solved.

A husband had killed his wife. The other murders were blamed on gang wars and no witnesses were willing to talk.

The following week, clips from the funeral of Rafe Wexford appeared on the local television news. People were shown arriving at the church, and footage inside the church showed where the sobbing widow sat. It was a deeply tragic scene. Derrick noticed his own mother dabbing at her eyes as uniformed soldiers who had served in Iraq with Rafe's father arrived. "There is nothing worse on this earth than losing a child," Derrick's mother said. "My heart goes out to that poor woman losing her child, especially in such a dreadful way."

As Derrick watched, his own heart ached. Then he noticed on the TV screen someone familiar sitting behind Mrs. Wexford. It was a young woman who graduated from Tubman High School last year—Bethany Walsh. Derrick knew her well because she had frequently babysat for Talia while she was a senior at Tubman. Derrick liked her and Talia absolutely loved her. She always played wonderful games with Talia and read her stories, so Talia didn't mind if her parents and older brothers and sister were all going out somewhere.

Derrick turned to his mother. "Mom, there's Beth—do you see her?"

"Oh my," Mom exclaimed. "She looks so different. But it *is* Bethany, bless her heart. I wonder how she knew the young man who died. Maybe she's a student at City College now too and they met there."

Bethany and her family used to live on Iroquois Street, but she moved away right after she graduated from Tubman. Derrick wondered if Bethany was the girlfriend of Rafe Wexford. She wasn't crying at the funeral, not in the clip anyway. But then people do their grieving in different ways. Bethany looked numb, like she had been struck by lightning or something.

Derrick was glad when they stopped showing scenes from the funeral and turned to other stories. Seeing the sad look on

Bethany Walsh's face only worsened his sense of guilt. Increasingly, Derrick was feeling like a bad person. He was helping cover up for a murderer.

But even when the newspeople moved on to other stories, Derrick's parents continued talking about the murder.

"I guess the police have nothing to go on," Pop suggested. "It's just another one of those awful killings when strangers kill strangers . . . and they're never solved."

"Yes," Mom responded, "seems like the only crimes they solve are when a relative does the killing. But these random murders, that's a whole other thing."

Derrick felt a chill go through his body. Had B.J. just killed a stranger? B.J. was into drugs, but he never ran with a gang. He wouldn't have killed Rafe Wexford because, say, he strayed into B.J.'s 'hood. B.J. had no territory. Or was Rafe not as clean as he appeared? Was he dealing too? Was it a drug deal gone bad? Maybe he sold B.J. some bad stuff. A lot of guys got killed

54

over something like that. Or maybe he bought from B.J. and stiffed him on the money. It seemed that's all B.J. cared about these days—money.

When Derrick got to school the next day, he heard Alonee saying, "I knew Bethany Walsh. I was a junior and she was a senior last year, but we were both cheerleaders. I haven't seen her in a long time, not since she graduated. But she was on TV last night at Rafe Wexford's funeral. She looks lots different, but I'm sure it was her."

"Yeah, I remember her," Jaris recalled. "She was really pretty. She looked haggard on TV though, like she hasn't been eating regular or something. Remember, she got kinda weird in the months before school was out? She started dating dropouts. She wasn't going with guys from Tubman anymore . . . I remember seeing her hanging out with some sleazeballs."

Alonee shook her head. "Poor Bethany. I'm not sure what happened. I saw her in the bathroom one time doing drugs. She got so scared. She told me she never did them before. She was, you know, just experimenting. But she'd come to school kinda spacey. Her grades were really good at the beginning of the year, but then they went south fast."

Sami Archer was standing nearby, wearing a T-shirt that read "Girl Power Means No Bad Dudes." "You guys talkin' about Bethany Walsh? Last time I seen her, I told her off. 'Girl,' I said to her, 'only a freakin' fool would be dating B.J. Brady like you doin'!'"

CHAPTER FOUR

Derrick was stunned. For a minute he thought he hadn't heard Sami right. He turned to her. "Sami, did you say Bethany Walsh was dating B.J. Brady?"

"I'm tellin' you, Derrick," Sami asserted, "I was blown out of my mind when she tol' me. She was goin' on and on about what a cool cat he was, and I go 'Girl, you need to get your head examined right now!' But she just laughed and that's the last I seen of her before the TV news last night."

Derrick, listening to this exchange, tried to understand B.J.'s girlfriend at Rafe Wexford's funeral? He couldn't make sense of it. Derrick wished he could talk to someone about all that happened, someone he could confide in. He desperately needed to share his terrible secret, but with whom? His parents would insist he go right to the police. All arguments would be useless. They would want him to do the right thing, never mind what might happen.

If Derrick refused to go to the police, then they would go and turn B.J. in. Derrick's friends would want him to go to the police too. But nobody else was there that night. They didn't see the coldness in B.J.'s eyes when he almost killed Derrick. Their families were not at risk. Derrick's family was. Derrick's parents, his brothers and sisters, everyone he loved was at risk.

He couldn't do rat out B.J. And he could talk with anyone, even though the secret was aching inside him and he felt ready to explode with its enormity.

"Derrick," Destini asked, coming up to him, "did you say you didn't have to work tonight? Want to go for pizza after school? They got a special on the pineapple topping that's so good. It's my treat."

"I couldn't let a girl buy my pizza," Derrick said.

"Oh come on, that's old stuff, Derrick," Destini chided him. "You guys got a big family and you're struggling. Mom and me are doing better. My pop left us some money when he died. It's made everything around our place a lot easier. It's not guys-buy-and-girls-take anymore. That's old. Whoever has the money pays and this time it's my treat. Come on, Derrick. Say yes. I like you."

No girl had ever told Derrick she liked him. Hearing that was a nice feeling, even though he was in such turmoil inside he couldn't appreciate it. "Okay," he agreed finally.

After school they walked over to the pizza place. Derrick felt strange walking with a pretty girl. He was always too embarrassed to ask a girl out. He thought she'd be insulted that a dumb guy like him had the nerve to want to be with her.

"I'm really proud to be with you, Destini," Derrick told her as they sat at a table.

"Oh go on," Destini objected. "I'm no big deal. I haven't had many boyfriends. I mean, just one and he was a loser. I always thought guys didn't like me. It seemed all the girls were getting dates ahead of me and I was freakin'. The guys would look at me and then they'd quick look at somebody else. Then this one guy, Tyron, well, he wasn't any good, but he did do something for me. He made me not so shy. Now I'm trying to be more like Sami. Man, do I admire that girl. She's nobody's fool. Sami is always asking guys out. And she gets asked too. She's hot, Derrick!" Destini giggled and said, "She's got chutzpah."

"What's chutzpah?" Derrick asked.

"Oh, that's like nerve," Destini explained. "Sami isn't afraid of anything, or anybody. She asks for what she wants."

"Yeah, she's like that," Derrick agreed. He knew what Sami would do if she had seen what happened in that alley. She would have been at the police station that same night. She would have marched into that police station and told them everything, and all B.J.'s threats would have meant nothing.

"So," Destini went on, "in English I looked over and saw you sitting there and I thought, 'Hey, why don't I ask him to go over for pizza?' I figured the worst that could happen is for you to say no, and that wouldn't have killed me. My mom always says what doesn't kill you makes you stronger."

Derrick liked the pizza, but he liked the girl more. She was so much fun to be with. She was easy to talk to. He told her all about his job and how he discouraged shoplifters with a gentle approach. "You don't have to be mean to people, even thieves," Derrick told her. "You just gotta let them know you know what they did and it'd be nice if they put the stuff back. But if they don't, well . . . you're not gonna bust them or anything."

"Derrick, that's amazing!" Destini said. "I always thought if they caught you stealing stuff, they'd call the cops and you'd be dragged off in handcuffs."

"Well, I guess that happens in some stores, but Wes doesn't want that," Derrick answered. "I like Wes. He's a great guy. He's from Iraq and he's been through some tough times. But it hasn't made him bitter or mean, you know. It like sorta made him nicer."

Derrick looked at the pretty girl before him and he thought how great it would be to confide in her, to pour out his heart, and to tell her his terrible secret. But he couldn't do that. He couldn't burden her with it. It wouldn't be fair. He was keeping a murderer's secret because he was afraid. He felt like a coward. But he couldn't put his heavy cross on Destini.

"We should go to the movies sometime," Destini suggested. "What time do you get off work?"

"About nine," Derrick replied. "We could catch a bus. I could stash my bike on the front of the bus in the rack."

"Yeah, my mom could drop me at the ninety-nine-cent store around eight when she's on her way to the hospital. My mom's a housekeeper at the hospital," Destini explained. "It'd be so much fun. There are so many good movies I'd love to see. Funny, romantic movies."

"Okay, we'll plan that," Derrick said. He was so excited about the turn of events that he almost forgot about B.J. Almost, but not quite.

When Derrick got his first paycheck from the 99¢ store, he turned most of it over to his parents, but he kept enough to take Destini to the movies and then someplace to eat. It would be the first time Derrick ever took a girl on a real date. Derrick also bought some small gifts for his brothers and sisters. He bought Kayla a pretty tank top she had been wanting, and he got Talia another outfit for her princess doll. Juno got a spaceship to go with his set, and Bruce got five dollars to spend on anything he wanted. Derrick felt like a big shot passing out gifts to his family.

On the Friday evening that Derrick was taking Destini out, he could think of nothing else. When he saw Destini's mother dropping her off outside the store, his heart raced. It was really happening. Derrick looked eagerly at the clock. It was ten minutes to quitting time.

"Hey Derrick," Wes called over to him. "Get out of here. You done enough work today, kid. I know what it's like to have a pretty girl on the string. Twenty years ago I had a pretty girl like that and now I'm married to her and she's given me four kids."

"Thanks, Wes," Derrick said. He rushed out and met Destini, then he pushed his bike toward the bus stop. When the bus came, Derrick loaded his bike on the front and climbed on to take a seat with Destini.

The movie turned out to be terrific, and they stopped at a little coffee shop and had crepes. It was almost eleven when the bus dropped Destini off at her corner. Derrick took his bike down, and he walked Destini to her door and waited for her to get inside safely.

"I had fun tonight," Destini told him.

"Me too," Derrick responded. He wondered if it would be all right to give Destini a little goodnight kiss. He was turning the question around and around in his mind as they lingered at her door. Suddenly Destini put her arms around Derrick's neck and kissed him, settling the issue. Then she went inside the duplex. Derrick waited until he heard her draw the latch across. Then he wheeled his bike back on the street. He had about a mile ride home to his place on Choctaw Street.

Derrick felt good. He had not felt this good since that terrible night. He was even thinking maybe the thing would somehow go away. He didn't know how, but tonight he was so happy he was willing to imagine that things could be good again.

Then he saw the red car on the street behind him. He told himself that it was just another red car, not B.J.'s Maserati. But as the car drew closer, Derrick saw that it was B.J. and he was close. Derrick almost jumped off his bike and began running, but it was too late. B.J. cruised up alongside him, coming to a screeching halt. "Don't freak, dude," B.J. shouted. "I just wanted to compliment you on that cute girlfriend you were hanging with tonight. She's got class man."

Destini! Now he knew about Destini too. That meant she was also in danger. If Derrick crossed B.J., he'd put not only his family in danger, but Destini too.

"I haven't said anything," Derrick croaked through a dry throat. He hated himself for his craven attitude.

"I know," B.J. assured him. "Take it easy man. You're doing fine. Everything is cool. You got a nice job at that ninety-nine-cent store, bringing in money for the family. Nice family, couple boys, two girls. That little sister, a really cute one. She five or six? She's wearing her braids nice and fancy. Now a girlfriend too. Pretty nice man. You got it made in the shade."

Derrick just stood there, chills going down his spine.

B.J. stepped out of the car and came toward Derrick. He held something in his hand. "Hey, just to show my appreciation, my man, here's a little something extra." He held out a crisp one hundred dollar bill.

"I don't want it," Derrick objected. Keeping quiet about the terrible crime was bad enough, but he couldn't accept blood money. He couldn't soil his hands on B.J.'s dirty money.

"Take it, man," B.J. urged, "or else I'm going to think you're having second thoughts about keeping our secret, y'hear what I'm saying?" B.J.'s voice turned sinister. "Take the bill dude, just to, you know, cement our relationship so to speak."

Derrick took the hundred dollar bill. He felt like vomiting. He stood there shaking with fear and humiliation. It had come to this. He had seen a murder and he was shielding the killer from justice. And now the murderer was paying him off. It was like they were partners in crime. The hundred dollars burned in Derrick's hand. The bill felt like a poisonous snake about to inject his body with venom.

"Well goodnight then, my man," B.J. hailed. "And good luck with the pretty little lady. May you live long and prosper." B.J. returned to his car and drove away.

"He knows just where I live," Derrick thought. "He knows I have two brothers and two sisters, one a little girl about five or six. He knows about Destini!" Derrick felt as if there was a noose around his neck that B.J. could draw tight anytime he felt like doing it.

On the upcoming weekend, a fishing trip was scheduled with the Tubman teenagers and a group of foster home kids they had already bonded with. Pastor Bromley from the local church had recruited the Tubman kids, including Derrick, Jaris, Trevor, Alonee, Sami, Kevin, and Destini. Derrick already had a bond with a little boy named Josh, who was expecting to see Derrick. Destini was very close to a little girl named Amber.

Derrick had learned that his young charge, Josh, had been bounced around several foster homes after his mother lost custody of him on charges of child neglect. Derrick liked Josh. He reminded him of his own brother, Juno. In spite of the troubles he had endured, Josh still had a friendly personality and a spirit of adventure.

Derrick, still troubled by his encounter with B.J., didn't feel like going on the trip, but he had made a commitment.

When they all arrived at the lake, the day was still overcast. "Great weather for fishing," Derrick assured Josh. Derrick and his own father took many fishing trips on the bay and at nearby lakes. These were some of the best times for Derrick. Before Derrick met Josh, the boy had never been fishing.

Some of the teenagers and their partners fished from a small pier that jutted into the lake, but Derrick and Josh went out in a small boat.

"I figure the bigger fish are out in the deeper water," Derrick told Josh. Derrick didn't know if that was true or not. Neither Derrick nor his father were good fishers. The fun of the fishing trip was in being outdoors, joking and laughing together, and barbecuing hot dogs over a fire pit.

"Derrick," Josh announced, a serious look on his face. "Somethin' goin' on in my classroom and I don't know what to do about it."

"What's goin' on dude?" Derrick asked. Out here on the lake, Derrick's own problems seemed to fade a little.

"Some kid in my class been stealin'. He takes money sometimes or stuff from lunches, and even he'll steal some trinket from a kid who's not looking," Josh explained. "I seen him, but nobody else has."

"You think the kid is stealing 'cause he's hungry and wants to trade stuff for food or something?" Derrick asked.

"No, 'cause he's got money. I see money in his pocket that he gets from home. He's got a regular mom and dad. They pack him big lunches with san'wiches and cookies and fruit too," Josh replied.

"Did you tell the teacher about what this kid is doing, Josh?" Derrick asked.

"No, 'cause this kid is real big, Derrick," Josh said. "He's lots bigger than me. He's bigger than just about anybody in class 'cause he was held back in school and he should be in seventh grade, not sixth like the rest of us. I'm scared of him, Derrick. I'm scared if I tell on him he'll beat me up."

Derrick got weak in the knees. He didn't need this kind of a problem in his life just now. It hit too close to home. Josh was covering up for a thirteen-year-old thief. Derrick was covering up for a murderer.

The motives were the same—fear.

"What'll I do, Derrick?" Josh asked. "I didn't, you know, know who to ask 'cepting for you, 'cause you're my friend. And you're a smart guy. I trust you, Derrick."

Derrick felt worse than ever. He didn't want to get Josh beaten up, but clearly the right thing to do was to report the kid who was stealing. But Derrick felt like a hypocrite to give the right advice. But he had to say something.

"Tell you what, Josh," Derrick sighed. "You find a time when you and your teacher are alone. Make sure this kid isn't around. You tell the teacher that he's been rippin' kids off, but you're afraid of him 'cause he's big and mean. Your teacher won't tell the bully it was you who reported him. Your teacher'll find a way to catch him and stop him."

Josh grinned. "Yeah! Our teacher's pretty cool. She won't tell on me. And she's smart too. When I tell her what this guy's been doing, she'll find a way to catch him. Wow, Derrick, I'm sure glad I got a friend like you. You're really smart!"

Derrick couldn't remember ever in his life before being called smart. Derrick knew it wasn't the truth but it was nice to hear anyway.

Josh's line jerked then.

"Josh! You got a bite," Derrick cried.

"Wow, a fish!" Josh yelled, pulling the line in.

When Josh saw that he'd caught a small, silvery fish, he said, "Awww, it's just a baby fish. Look how he's fightin', Derrick. Let's throw him back."

"Yeah," Derrick agreed, taking hold of the hook and prying it as gently as he could from the fish's mouth. He flipped the fish back into the lake.

"Will he be okay, Derrick?" Josh asked.

Derrick smiled at the boy. "Yeah, he'll be fine. And I got to say I admire you, Josh. You didn't want to take no little half-grown fish from the lake. That's being a real sportsman."

They rowed in to shore then and joined the others at the barbecue. The smell of roasting hotdogs and hamburgers filled the air. Derrick smiled over at Destini, who was sitting close to Amber as they giggled together. Derrick decided this was a good place to be and a fine thing they were doing.

When Derrick got back from the fishing trip, he was tired, but he'd had a lot of fun with Josh. They were already planning the next trip, next time to the aquarium, and Josh was looking forward to seeing the sharks.

Derrick felt sorry for Josh. Unlike Derrick, he didn't have loving parents and brothers and sisters. Derrick loved both his parents and he knew they loved him. He couldn't imagine what life was like for kids like Josh who didn't have a mom to fuss over them and a pop to teach them the ropes. Derrick made up his mind to stick with Pastor Bromley's program and to continue his friendship with Josh as long as the boy needed him.

CHAPTER FIVE

On Saturday, Derrick went to work at the 99¢ And More store, and he gently discouraged two ten-year-olds from stealing sports cards. Then, as he was straightening up the shelves, Wes once again complimented him on his hard work. When Derrick quit work at nine, he noticed a black pickup truck parked out front. He'd never seen the pickup before, but he could tell that a girl sat at the wheel. She looked right at Derrick as he came out of the store and unlocked his bicycle.

The girl got out of the truck and walked toward him. "Hi Derrick," she called. The voice was familiar but he didn't recognize her in the darkness.

"Hello," Derrick answered. "Do I know you?"

"I'm Bethany Walsh," she told him. "Derrick, could you toss your bike in the bed of the truck and come have a cup of coffee with me? I need to talk to you."

Derrick stared at the girl. She was much thinner than the Bethany Walsh who babysat his little sister. She looked haggard and sick.

Derrick thought for a minute that B.J. had sent this girl, that he was hiding in the truck somewhere, and that he'd jump Derrick when he got in. But he didn't see anybody but the girl. Still, what if she planned to drive him to some lonely spot where B.J. was waiting . . .

"What do you want?" Derrick asked her.

"Just to go down to that drive-in down the road, and get some coffee and talk, Derrick," she replied.

"You were at the funeral of that guy who was shot, Rafe Wexford. When they showed pictures of the funeral I saw you,"

Derrick told her, as he put his bike into the back of the truck. He opened the door to the passenger side of the pickup and got in.

"Oh my God, did they show me on TV?" Bethany said with a shudder. She started the engine.

"Uh . . . was he your boyfriend or something?" Derrick asked. Was Rafe one of the weird boyfriends Bethany started dating on her downhill slide after graduating from Tubman?

"Yeah, he and I dated for a while," Bethany answered. "I was dating a lot of guys. I went to clubs and I got friends off the Internet too."

"I'm real sorry what happened to him, you know," Derrick told her. "If you cared about him, it must've been hard." His mouth was drying up. He was nervous. He glanced at Bethany's arms and he saw evidence of needles. It made him sick and sad.

They pulled into a small hamburger joint and ordered a coffee and a soda at the drive-through window. When they got their drinks, Bethany drove to the extreme far end of the parking lot. "Derrick," Bethany said, "when I was babysitting your little sister, I always thought you were a nice guy. I mean, you were always so kind to everybody, so polite."

"Thanks, I guess," Derrick said, sipping his soda.

"Looking back on it now," Bethany started to say, "I wish we had gotten together, you and me. It all might have been different. But you seemed kind of dull. You were, you know, too good to be true. I wanted a little more excitement. I guess I liked bad boys."

"Some girls do," Derrick replied.

"I got an apartment across town with two other girls," Bethany went on. "We got waitress jobs and when we weren't working, we were partying all the time. It was amazing. I was free. No parents telling me when to come home, asking me questions. Nobody hassling me."

Derrick continued to drink the soda. He was wondering where all this was leading.

"Yeah well," he said, "I never wanted too much excitement. It's okay with me if things just go along okay . . . not a lot of bumps in the road."

"I met Rafe at a club," Bethany told him with a forlorn sigh. "He was so handsome and a really good athlete. I guess you could see that from the pictures they showed of him on TV."

Derrick felt nausea sweeping him. He saw the face on the pavement, against the garbage pail in the alley. He remembered the blood running down the side of his face. Derrick feared that as long as he lived—if he got to be ninety years old—he would never forget that face turning cold and hard in the alley.

"Rafe was a real straight shooter," Bethany went on. "I liked him and he was mad about me, Derrick. He really fell for me. I'm tellin' you, he was texting me like thirty times a day. He was sending me flowers and . . . it got to be too much. I just didn't have it for him like he did for me.

I thought 'I'm eighteen years old' and I want to just have fun. I wasn't ready for a collar and a leash, but he was like wanting me all the time."

"Poor guy," Derrick thought. "Poor fool."

"I was into bad things, Derrick," Bethany was saying. "Drugs. Pills. Then worse. I hung out with wild guys . . . I guess some of them were freaks. Well, I fell in love with one of the freaks. I felt different with him than I did with Rafe. This guy I was in love with. I never knew what it was like to love someone like I loved him. I was doing coke and I sold some . . . he was selling junk too. We were on this crazy awesome trip that never ended. It was B.J. Brady."

"You dumped Rafe for B.J.?" Derrick asked.

"Yeah," Bethany nodded. "Being with B.J. is like being at an amusement park twenty-four-seven. Well, you know the kind of guy he is. You knew him as a kid, right? He loved me . . . no, he *loves* me. As much as I love him."

"You're still with him then," Derrick inquired. "So why did you go to the other guy's funeral?"

"Guilt, I guess," Bethany answered. "Derrick"—she had a terrible look on her face now, and she was shaking—"I know everything that happened." She put her hand on Derrick's knee, "I mean *everything*, about you being there and seeing it all . . ."

B.J. told her. He had to have told her. Derrick's mind was a blur of fear and shock. What was this all about? Why was she here talking to him?

"Derrick," Bethany kept talking, "you need to know why it happened. I'm so sorry a good guy like you got mixed up in this. You didn't ask for it. You don't deserve it. It was one of those rotten things that just happen. But, see, maybe it'll help you if you know why it happened. See, it just about killed Rafe when I ditched him for B.J. He was crushed and heartbroken. Then he was mad."

"Did Rafe hurt you or something?" Derrick asked.

"No. He never would have done that. But he found out I'd sold crack. He got the goods on me. He came over to Papa's Pool Hall one night when I was there with B.J. I'd never seen Rafe like that. He was cold and calm. His eyes were like chunks of ice. 'Bethany,' he goes, 'I'm turning you in to the cops. I can promise you you'll go to prison for a long time. You'll be rotting in some women's prison, growing old. No parties, no boyfriends. You won't get the chance to break another guy's heart. You'll get old and ugly before they let you out, girl . . .' "

"When did this happen?" Derrick gasped.

"Just before that night, Derrick," Bethany answered, crying now. "After Rafe left, I was hysterical. I collapsed into B.J.'s arms. I know Rafe could do what he threatened. He was going to punish me good for dumping him . . ."

"So B.J. killed him because of that?" Derrick asked.

"B.J. tricked him into coming to that alley. I think B.J. told him I'd be there and

82

I changed my mind and I still loved Rafe . . . but B.J. thought it was the only way to save me from prison. I'm so sorry you were there, Derrick. I know B.J. made you swear not to tell what you saw . . . I know how horrible it must be for you."

"Does B.J. know you came here tonight to talk to me?" Derrick asked.

"No. I did it on my own," Bethany shook her head, "but he wouldn't care. I came here for *your* sake, Derrick. I didn't want you to think that was some random murder that night. It must be terrible to have to keep quiet about seeing a murder . . . and I know you're scared for yourself and your family. But I thought if you knew *why* he did it, it'd make it easier. I'm not saying what B.J. did was right. It was horrible and evil. I'm haunted by it too, Derrick. I let Rafe love me, and then I two-timed him and because of me he died . . . I'm an evil person, Derrick, and I don't even deserve to live."

"No, don't say that," Derrick said. "You didn't know what would happen."

"I've made a mess of everything, Derrick," Bethany protested. "B.J. has done a lot of bad things, but he never killed anyone before. He did it for me. He loves me. He told me I'm the only person in his whole life who ever really loved him. His parents didn't even love him. They tossed him out. He did that terrible thing because of his love for me, Derrick."

Derrick looked at the girl, remembering the fresh-faced teenager playing games with his little sister only last year. She seemed to have aged at least ten years.

"You still wanna be with him, huh?" Derrick said.

Tears started at the corners of her eyes and ran down her hollowed cheeks. "Yeah," she admitted. "I still love him. I'm sick and horrified by what he did, but he didn't know any other way to save me from prison. They go really hard on crack dealers. Oh, Derrick, I wish it was last year again and I was babysitting Talia. It was such a happy time. I don't know how all this happened. B.J. has an excuse. He's had a rotten life. But I had good parents and a nice home . . . why did I do this?"

"Do you still talk to your parents?" Derrick asked her.

"I call them sometimes . . . I send emails," she replied. "I send Mom flowers on Mother's Day. I tell them I'm fine. I tell them I'll see them soon, but I know I won't. I don't ever want them to see me like this. Look at me. I look like some spook . . ."

Derrick drained his soda. He sat there silently for a few minutes, then he said, "Bethany, you could go to rehab. You could get help."

"I've been *selling*," she insisted.

"Bethany, there's gotta be a way out of this," Derrick protested.

"I'm sticking with B.J. wherever that takes me," Bethany said. She started the pickup. "I'll drop you home. Your parents are probably worried about you. You got good parents, Derrick. A good family."

At his home, Derrick pulled his bike from the back of Bethany's pickup and rolled it into the garage.

"Everything okay, child?" Mom asked when he came in. "It's getting late. I thought somethin' mighta gone wrong."

"No, Mom," Derrick assured his mom, "everything is okay at the store. We just worked a little longer." He went to his room and flopped down on the bed. The small Shaw apartment had three bedrooms for the seven of them. Derrick's parents had the smallest bedroom. The next in size was divided by curtains into bedrooms for Kayla and Talia. The largest bedroom was divided into three little cells, one for each of the boys. There was hardly enough room to turn around, but the arrangement worked.

Derrick remembered the hundred dollar bill B.J. had given him, still in his wallet. He had about five crinkled dollar bills of his own, and the crisp hundred. There was no way Derrick could spend that money. He couldn't keep it either. It made him sick to know it was there, offering more evidence of his own moral cowardice.

Derrick thought about Pastor Bromley's youth group and how they were always scrimping for money to pay for outings for the kids. The camping trips required gear and movies meant ticket money. A treat at the ice cream store was expensive. Derrick thought about his young friend Josh, who had a series of foster homes and not much fun in his life. All the kids in the group got there because they had run out of families and run out of luck. Derrick came to a conclusion about what he would do with the dirty hundred dollar bill and then he was finally able to fall asleep around midnight.

On Sunday morning, Derrick surprised his parents by wanting to go to church with them. Kayla, Talia, and Juno went every Sunday to Bible classes, and Bruce often went, but Derrick wasn't too good about going. Derrick sat through Pastor Bromley's sermon about the Good Shepherd. Then, after services, Derrick cornered Pastor Bromley and said, "I got me a moral problem."

The pastor nodded gravely and said, "I'm listening, Derrick."

"A bad man gave me some money. He didn't ask me to do anything wrong with the money, but I can't spend it. I'm part of that group with the foster kids and—" Derrick began to say.

"Yes Derrick, I see you with young Josh. He really likes you. Already it's helping the boy," Pastor Bromley said.

"I want to give the money to that program, for the kids, to pay for trips and stuff," Derrick told the pastor, pulling the hundred from his wallet and handing it to him.

"Why thank you, Derrick," Pastor Bromley said. "We'll put this to good use for the children. As for the bad man, pray for him."

"This is just between you and me," Derrick went on. "I wouldn't want my parents to know . . . okay?"

"Of course," the pastor assured him.

As the family drove home to Choctaw Street, Derrick's father smiled and said, "I saw you having a heart-to-heart talk with the pastor, Derrick. I'm glad to see you are turning to the church for spiritual guidance. The pastor is a very wise man."

"Yeah, he is," Derrick replied, glad that the dirty money was gone from his wallet.

"Mommy, what's a shepherd?" Talia asked.

"A shepherd is somebody who takes care of others," Mom answered. "In the Bible it sometimes meant the man who took care of the sheep. But it can be anybody who guides others. Like Pastor Bromley is like a shepherd to us. And your brother, Derrick, he and his friends are like shepherds to those dear children from the foster homes. They lead the children on trips and guide them." Mom smiled warmly at Derrick. She was very proud of his work with the foster children.

Derrick realized that he was a very good kid. He never gave his family any trouble.

He couldn't remember a teacher sending home a note that he had done something wrong. There were plenty notes about how slow he was in his schoolwork, but never any discipline problems. Derrick was a good boy, as Bethany had said. "You seemed kind of dull," she had said.

Derrick never had a serious relationship with a girl, maybe because he was dull. He thought that just might be it. But now he thought, with deep sadness, that he was no longer even a good kid. A good kid would not be covering up for a murderer. If his parents knew what he was hiding, they would be bitterly disappointed.

Derrick was studying hard for an upcoming English test all week, and when he went to school and took the test, he felt good about it. He wrote a pretty good essay on a hard story—"The Guest" by Albert Camus. He had read the story over and over until he thought he understood it. In the story, a schoolteacher was ordered to take a man who had murdered his cousin to the police station.

He wanted nothing to do with it. Finally, the teacher gave the murderer a package of food and some money, told him to walk to the police station, and turn himself in. Derrick sympathized with the teacher in the story. He was caught up in a moral problem he didn't want. Just like Derrick.

Derrick was pleased with his performance on the test, and his spirits were a little better when he left the classroom until he saw Destini. She looked like she had been crying. Derrick caught up to her and said, "Destini, are you all right?"

"Yeah, I'm fine, just fine!" Destini spat out the words like they were bitter in her mouth. She turned away from Derrick. He ran to keep pace with her brisk walk. She was acting as if she hated Derrick and wanted to lose him.

"Destini, what's the matter?" Derrick asked her. "What happened? Why are you acting like this?"

"It's stupid," Destini snapped. "I mean it's just stupid. I mean, we're not even dating.

We had one lousy date. A movie and those crepes. What was *that*? Big deal. It's all totally stupid. *I'm totally stupid*."

"Destini," Derrick groaned, "we had a good time. It was one of the best times I ever had. What's the matter with you? What did I do wrong? You're mad at me and I don't even know what I did wrong."

"It's none of my business," Destini said. "Am I so desperate for a boyfriend that I latch onto a guy after one stupid date? Do I think he's my boyfriend because we went to a stupid movie? What makes me think he's not going to look at other girls and go out with other girls? I must be crazy. I'm tellin' you, I'm going to forget boys entirely. Mom is right. I am never going to have a boyfriend and that's just fine with me."

"Destini, I don't get any of this," Derrick exclaimed. "I know I'm not real sharp but I don't understand any of what's going on. I wish you'd tell me so I could understand."

"I'm going to be a single woman who has absolutely no social life because going out with guys is the most stupid thing in the whole world," Destini cried.

"Destini, please!" Derrick pleaded. "I'm doing my best to get this. I am totally confused. Just tell me what I did wrong and I'll try to fix it, 'cause I really do like you and I wouldn't have hurt your feelings on purpose."

Finally Destini stopped walking. She looked up at Derrick, her eyes teary again. "I was getting to *like* you too, Derrick. I thought we liked each other and everything was going along good. Then this girl, she's a friend of Jasmine's, she saw you on a date with another girl on Saturday night. And like Jaz just couldn't wait to tell me. I mean, she *loves* to bring bad news."

"No. No!," Derrick protested. "That wasn't a date."

"Jaz said her friend saw you and this girl sitting together in a pickup truck," Destini sobbed, "and you looked real cozy and it was like you were looking into her eyes and she was looking into yours." Destini tossed her head, angry more at herself than at Derrick. "It's not your fault, Derrick. It's my fault. I read too much into that stupid date that wasn't anything. You've got every right to date any girl you want and sit with her in the dark and do whatever you were doing. I'm not mad at you, Derrick. I'm mad at me!"

"She *wasn't* a girlfriend, Destini. She wasn't my girlfriend," Derrick asserted.

"You don't owe me an explanation, Derrick. Honest you don't," Destini said.

"Destini, please shut up for a minute, okay?" Derrick said desperately. "I mean if you don't shut up for one little minute I can't explain, okay? . . . This girl was the girlfriend of the guy who was murdered in the alley. She used to babysit for my family. She just needed to talk to somebody is all . . ."

CHAPTER SIX

Destini said nothing. Her eyes became unusually large, and tears splashed off her long eyelashes, the ones she'd taken great pains to curl last night. "Ohhh Derrick," she moaned. "I am so sorry. I am so incredibly stupid and selfish. The whole world revolves around stupid, selfish Destini Fletcher, and nobody else has a right to exist. That poor girl. She must be in total shock. And leave it to you to offer a shoulder to cry on. Oh Derrick, you are so sweet and kind. I don't know how you put up with me!"

"No, no, it's okay," Derrick said. "It was just a misunderstanding. This girl, her name is Bethany Walsh and she used to babysit for my little sister Tali before she graduated from Tubman. She saw me at the ninety-nine-cent store and just asked if we could get some coffee and, you know talk about stuff. It was sad."

"Wow, and I'm all wrapped up in my petty stuff," Destini sniffed. "I must make you sick, Derrick."

"No, you make me happy, Destini," Derrick told her. "Honest. It just makes me so glad that you care enough for me to get so mad about nothing,. Maybe we can go somewhere on Sunday, to the beach or something."

Destini gave Derrick a hug. "I'm crazy about you," she giggled.

Derrick found out in the afternoon that Jasmine hadn't told just Destini about Derrick being in the pickup truck with Bethany. She had told half the junior class. At lunch, Jaris and Trevor came over to where Derrick was eating with Destini and Alonee. Jaris gave Derrick a funny look and said, "Hey dude, what's with you and that chick, Bethany Walsh?"

"Nothing," Derrick sighed. "She used to babysit for my family when she was at Tubman and she saw me in the ninety-nine-cent store and wanted to talk. She was kinda close to the guy who got murdered in the alley and she's all messed up."

Sami Archer came over and jumped into the conversation. "Boy," she told Derrick, "that girl wasn't goin' with Rafe Wexford when he was killed. You know what dude put his brand on her hide? She belongs to B.J. Brady. I don't know what kinda smoke she was blowin' in your face, but she's poison. She got on drugs even when she was goin' here. She got outta her parents' nest just as soon as she could, 'cause this little bird wanted to fly and I don't mean in a seven-forty-seven."

"I'd put a lot of space between me and her if I was you, Derrick," Alonee advised. "B.J.'s dangerous. I hear stuff about him that gives me the chills."

"It was just a one-time thing," Derrick said nervously. "I won't be seeing her again."

"That sounds like a good plan," Sami affirmed.

Derrick wanted to change the subject. He was terrified that somebody would connect the dots and link B.J. Brady to Rafe's death. Then it might get back to B.J. that Derrick was responsible for the connection.

"That was a good English test," Derrick said. "I studied hard and I think I did better than I ever did in Pippin's class."

"Yeah, I did okay too," Jaris said.

At the end of the lunch period, everybody drifted off to their classes, but Jaris stayed behind. He approached Derrick, his expression almost grim. "Dude, you're not mixed up in something over your head, are you?" he asked.

"No way," Derrick lied.

"You've been looking stressed, man. I've been noticing that for a while now . . . ever since that dude got wasted in the alley," Jaris went on.

"No, no," Derrick protested desperately. "It's just that I'm starting that new job and I been studying real hard to bring up my grades and stuff, and you know I sorta have a girlfriend now . . . Destini Fletcher. Lot of stuff goin' on in my life."

"Derrick, listen up," Jaris directed. "If there's anything that ever gets too tense to handle by yourself, you come over and talk to me, okay? You hear what I'm saying bro? You know I got your back man. We've been the three musketeers for a long time now— you, me, and Trev. Nothing we can't handle. Don't ever think you got to take it on alone, you hear me?"

"Yeah Jaris, thanks," Derrick nodded.

Derrick walked away from the conversation both comforted and frightened. Jaris had no idea of what Derrick was dealing with—that he was an eyewitness to murder. Derrick could only imagine how shocked and disbelieving Jaris would be if he knew the truth.

The next day there was an article in the newspaper about Rafe Wexford's murder. Derrick read it anxiously.

"Police Sift Clues in College Student Murder," the headline read. Inside the article, the reporter said many tips were coming in. Derrick's hopes rose that somebody else had witnessed the shooting, not just him. He hoped it would be clear that several people had seen it, so B.J. would not zero in on Derrick. The article also said the police were seeking several "persons of interest" for questioning.

Bruce saw his brother reading the article. "What's it say?" Bruce asked. "The cops gonna solve that murder pretty soon, Derrick?"

"They're just looking into clues," Derrick answered.

"I bet it turns out to be gangbangers," Bruce said. "Those dudes shoot each other over nothing. One guy looks at another guy wrong, and that's it. He's dead. Maybe that poor dude just looked funny at one of the gangbangers." Bruce paused then and stared at his brother, "You okay, Derrick?"

"Yeah, I'm okay, little brother. Why you ask?" Derrick responded.

"Used to be nighttimes, you'd sleep like a stone man," Bruce said. "You'd hit that pillow and you'd be out cold. Now I hear you tossing around all night like you can't sleep. I'm right there on the other side of that partition dude. I hear those bed springs squeakin' and groanin' most of the night.

Derrick smiled and tired to make a joke of it. "You just wait till you're sixteen like me, little brother. You won't sleep so good either."

"You got girlfriend problems, I bet," Bruce said with a sly grin.

Derrick decided Bruce might as well attribute his brother's restlessness to that. "You just a baby, Bruce," Derrick told him. "You're fourteen. You don't know what's goin' down. I'm sixteen. I got me a man's problems. Yeah, I got a girlfriend and that's a problem all right.".

That evening, Derrick was outside oiling his bike when the sleek red car zoomed by.

"Whoa man," Bruce gasped. "Did you see those wheels, Derrick? That was a Maserati man. Wow, that's some car. I'd sure like wheels like that when I get older. Man, I'd own the world!"

Derrick felt the blood run from his legs. He was numb all over. Why was B.J. cruising by the apartment on Choctaw Street? Did he suspect something? Did he think he'd see police cruisers parked in front of Derrick's place with the cops taking a statement or something? Or was B.J. just trying to stiffen Derrick's resolve? Was B.J. sending a reminder that he knew just where the Shaw family lived and that, if Derrick crossed him . . . ?

Derrick's father was suddenly standing there, as the Maserati turned around and came back, cruising slowly down Choctaw. "That's B.J. Brady," Pop said bitterly. "Look at him, flaunting his dirty way of life in front of decent people. Rotten drug dealer."

Derrick said nothing. He put more oil on his bike. Then finally Derrick said, "Don't pay any attention to him, Pop."

"That's how come he's gotten so rich, Derrick. We ain't payin' no attention to him," Pop declared. "He's just laughin' in the faces of respectable folks. You know what he's after, don't you? He's wanting to show off what a fine car he got, and all the gold chains and the money, and he's hopin' he can recruit the young ones. The youngsters get tempted and fall in with him. A young boy gonna look at that man in his Maserati and say, 'Look at all he got and he don't even work up a sweat. Me. I'm slaving away at the car wash for squat!' "

Bruce was paying little attention to what his father was saying. His eyes were still full of the Maserati. "How much you figure something like that costs?" Bruce asked. "The car I mean."

"That man drivin' the car is a drug dealer, son," Pop said. "He sells poison to people and their lives go down the drain.

103

You see these little babies wandering the streets because their mamas are home stoned and haven't sense enough to mind them? That's from drugs. You see these boys stumbling around the gutter with no future? That's from scum like B.J. Brady. He oughta be in prison and someday he will be." With that, Pop turned and stomped back in the house.

Derrick rolled his bike into the garage. As he was heading into the apartment, Mom came to the door and yelled out, "They got a suspect in the murder of that boy. It's on the TV now."

Derrick rushed into the house and watched the TV along with Bruce and their father. The local news reporter was talking in an excited voice.

"Police are talking to local gang member Fabian Rogers in connection with the murder of Rafe Wexford. The eighteen-year-old is a member of the Nite Ryders gang, which has long been a source of violence on Grant Avenue. No charges have yet been filed against Rogers, but the police are investigating reports of serious bad blood between him and the murdered college student."

Derrick stared, stunned at the television screen.

The police had the wrong guy! They were questioning the wrong guy. Derrick never dreamed something like this could happen. It was his worst nightmare come true. It was bad enough covering up for a murderer, but how could he remain silent while an innocent kid took the fall?

The phone rang for Derrick. When he picked it up, it was Sami Archer. She sounded like she was crying. "Derrick," Sami cried, "you got the TV on? The police arrested my cousin Fabian! That boy didn't do no murder. My Aunt Clare is losin' it, Derrick!"

"Yeah I just heard," Derrick replied. "It's a stupid mistake. They'll let him go, Sami."

"Fabian's sister, Latasha," Sami said, "she's in our junior class, Derrick. That poor child is cryin' her eyes out. Fabian kinda wild and he's been in trouble, but nothin' big. Worst he ever done was taggin'. I called up my uncle, the cop, and I told him those guys down there must be crazy to think Fabian did this. He told me to mind my own business, that the cops know what they're doin', but you know how that goes. The cops all stick together."

"Don't worry, Sami, they'll straighten it out," Derrick assured her. His heart was pounding. Guilt washed over him like dark waves.

"They got a lot of pressure on this deal," Sami wailed. "Rafe Wexford's daddy's big war hero. Now Rafe's mom left with no child. They got to nail somebody, *anybody*."

"They'll hold him for a few hours and then they'll see it was a mistake," Derrick said. Derrick felt sick. He reassured Sami as best he could and then hung up. He didn't know Latasha well, but he always saw her sitting dutifully in English, taking notes.

Fabian, her brother, had dropped out of the senior class, but his family was trying to get him his high school certificate.

"Well," Pop sighed, looking at the TV. "The boy *is* a gangbanger. That don't say much good about him. He mighta had an argument with the boy who died. Doesn't take much to set them off."

"I can't believe Fabian Rogers would kill somebody," Mom said. "He's Sami Archer's cousin." Derrick's mother had a sorrowful look on her face. "That poor mother, Lidey Rogers. She sings with me in the Praise choir at church. She and her husband struggling to keep their children on the right track. She loves her children same as I do. Lord in Heaven, I hope this isn't true. How brokenhearted she must be right now. I'm going to give her a call and tell her we're prayin' for her and the boy, and if they need anything, we're here for them." Within minutes, Derrick heard his mother on the phone sympathizing with Mrs. Rogers.

"*Fabian is innocent*." Those words kept going through Derrick's mind. The guy was innocent, and they were questioning him for murder. He must be half crazy with fear. Derrick thought—that kid, that family— they're all going through fire and it's not right.

In school the next day everyone gathered around Latasha Rogers, giving her hugs and encouragement. Her parents decided to send her to school in spite of what was happening because she needed support and that's where her friends were.

"My brother would never hurt some-body," Latasha was sobbing. "It's all because of that stupid thing that happened in traffic."

"What happened?" Alonee asked.

"Right before that guy got killed," Latasha gasped between sobs. "My brother was driving on the freeway and this guy cut him off. Fabian, he honked his horn and yelled some stuff, and they both got off the freeway and . . . They parked and they were yelling at each other, and this

Wexford guy claimed Fabian threatened him with a screwdriver or something. Fabian has a big mouth, but he'd never hurt anybody. Anyway, Wexford, he reported the thing to the police. He got Fabian's license and stuff . . . the same night . . . Rafe Wexford was killed . . . it was a horrible coincidence."

Alonee shook her head sadly.

"They don't have enough to hold him," Trevor said. "They'd need a murder weapon or a witness."

Derrick could think of nothing but his own guilt in all this. If he had done his duty, B.J. would now be in police custody and none of this would be happening. B.J.'s threats against Derrick and his family echoed in Derrick's tortured brain.

Derrick wondered now if he came forward with what he saw, would the police even believe him? Wouldn't they wonder why he had waited so long? Derrick could imagine himself in court at B.J.'s trial, with B.J.'s clever lawyers ripping him apart.

Derrick knew he wasn't clever enough to outwit lawyers who made thousands of dollars a day. He played an imaginary script in his head.

"Derrick Shaw, you say you witnessed the murder of Rafe Wexford?"

"Yes sir."

"And you said nothing for days, even weeks? You witnessed a brutal murder and you just kept it to yourself? Do you expect the court to believe that?"

"I was scared. B.J. threatened me and made me promise not to say anything in exchange for him not shooting me."

"You saw a fine young man get murdered and you went home and slept like a baby, Derrick Shaw? What kind of a human being are you? Or is the story you now tell us a lie? Did you perhaps just imagine you witnessed B.J. Brady shoot Rafe Wexford? Isn't that the real truth, Derrick Shaw?"

"No, no, I really saw him shoot this guy in the alley."

"But it was dark. How could you have seen anything?"

"I did. I saw B.J. Brady shoot and kill Rafe Wexford. I should have come and told you right away. But I was scared. You've got to believe me . . . I was scared."

"You are telling the court that B.J. Brady shot this young man and you witnessed it, and then for some reason Brady spared your life? You witnessed him commit murder and yet he let you live? Why would somebody who had just committed cold-blooded murder permit a witness to his crime go free to point the finger at him. Can you tell us that, Derrick Shaw?"

"I don't know why that happened. I don't know. I guess there's some good even in bad people."

"Isn't it true, Derrick Shaw that you saw nothing at all that night and now you are before this court spinning a fantasy and implicating an innocent man, B.J. Brady, in a crime he did not commit? Isn't that true, Derrick Shaw?"

"No, no . . ."

"That's all, Derrick Shaw. You may be excused."

And then B.J. Brady would be found innocent, but he would know that Derrick had gone against his sworn promise. B.J. Brady would be walking free, free to take his revenge whenever it suited him.

The end of the script would be just a matter of time. A shattered front window on Choctaw Street. A rifle shot. Derrick dead on the floor. Or Mom, or Pop, or Bruce, or even little Talia.

It would be payback time.

CHAPTER SEVEN

I'll tell Jaris," Derrick thought. "He said I should come talk to him if the burden is too heavy. He's a smart guy. He's a good guy too. He'll know what to do."

But inside Derrick's brain came another, taunting voice. "Jaris can't help you, fool. Nobody can. If you cross B.J., it's over. Nobody can help you. The cops can't watch you twenty-four-seven. And what about your family? You're on your own, Derrick Shaw. You are all alone."

When Derrick went to work at the 99¢ store, he told Wes he thought the police had the wrong man for the Wexford killing. "I know that Fabian guy and his family," Derrick told Wes. "I can't believe they think he did it." Derrick shook his head and added, "It's not fair."

Wes shrugged his shoulders. Back in Iraq when he was Waleed, you stopped asking what was fair and what wasn't. Nothing was fair. The people in the bazaars who got blown to pieces had done nothing except wanting to buy food for their families. People were arrested for no reason. People disappeared. "Fair" was not a word that intelligent people used anymore. Maybe, Wes thought, "fair" was not a word that mattered much anymore anywhere. Wes looked at the boy who seemed terribly upset. He was so young. He still believed in fairness, so Wes tried to comfort him. "Derrick, if this kid is innocent, they'll let him go. He'll be okay," Wes assured him. Wes didn't really believe that, but he said it to console the kid he liked very much and who was the best employee he ever had.

"I hope so," Derrick said, not believing Wes's words either but clinging to them as a drowning man clings to a rotten board from a doomed ship until it too sinks beneath the waves into the icy graveyard of the sea.

The customers came and went, and then, to Derrick's surprise, Bethany Walsh walked in. She found Derrick sweeping in a corner and said very softly, "Don't freak over what happened, Derrick."

"An innocent guy is going down for B.J.," Derrick shot back. "It's killin' me girl."

"No, no," Bethany protested, "it's just a fluke. That guy will be out of jail in no time."

"The family is poor. They can't even afford a good lawyer," Derrick said.

"They can't keep him longer than forty-eight hours if they got no evidence," Bethany declared. "And they couldn't have evidence, right?"

"Some guy on TV said they can get the court's okay, then keep people longer while they dig for more stuff," Derrick countered.

"He'll be out of jail today, Derrick," Bethany said. She looked worried. To her, Derrick didn't look good. He looked like he was breaking under the strain.

"You think I'm a stupid fool, Bethany," Derrick told her. "Maybe I am, but I know when somebody is blowing smoke. B.J. is dancing in the streets that another poor guy is gonna take the fall for what he did."

"Take it easy," Bethany tried to calm him. "You don't understand B.J. I do. I think you have to love somebody to really understand them. He's not all bad, Derrick. He doesn't want this kid on the hook. Believe me, it's going to be okay. Just hang in there."

It came over the television news that Fabian was still in police custody that night. The TV station had a special report on gang violence. Fabian was a gang member, and when you watched the report, you believed any gangbanger was capable of murder, including Fabian. Terrible past incidents of violence, blamed on the Nite Ryders and other local gangs, were revisited. It was a very powerful case against Fabian Rogers.

Ever since the night of the murder, Derrick found it hard to sleep. Before that night, he was asleep when his head hit the pillow. Mom always said he was the soundest sleeper she ever knew.

"Boy, if the end of the world was a-comin', you'd sleep right through it," Mom would joke.

All through those sleepless nights, Derrick saw Rafe Wexford's face — the heartrending sight of a human being whose life was draining out of him. Sometimes the awful vision would speak to Derrick.

"I'm dead man. Would you close my eyes for me?" he'd beg. "Just do that for me."

Derrick knew with dreadful certainty that, as long as he lived, the dead man would cry out to him for justice and he would have no peace. It didn't matter why B.J. had killed him. Maybe he did it out of a twisted sense of love for his girlfriend, but it didn't matter in the end. He took a life. He committed murder. That wrong could not stand.

Then, one night it all poured out of Derrick, as if he had to throw up something bad from his stomach. Derrick had been too terrified to go to the police. Every night, the fears had swirled around his head like a whirlpool of dark water pulling him deeper into an abyss. That night, he was having trouble breathing. And then he began to sob. At first the sobs were soft, but they grew into intense, racking spasms of sorrow. He couldn't stop. He was drenched in perspiration, and his blankets were wound around him like wraps on a mummy.

Mom and Pop came into his tiny bedroom. They told the two other boys to leave them alone until they found out what was wrong with Derrick. Pop stood alongside the bed, but Mom sat on the bed, gathering Derrick in her arms as she used to do when he was small, having bad dreams. "Baby . . . what's wrong?" she asked. "Tell us what's wrong."

Derrick told them everything. He told them about being in the alley and seeing B.J. kill Rafe Wexford. He told them that B.J. was about to kill him too, but he begged for his life and swore he'd never tell what he saw. So B.J. let him go.

"He said he'd hurt you too if I told," Derrick wept.

Derrick's mother rocked him in her arms. "It's all right, baby," Mom purred to her son. "Don't you worry. It's gonna be all right. We all gonna stick together and help you fix this, son. All of us together. We must go and tell the police the whole thing."

Pop nodded. "In the morning we all goin' down to the police station, son. It's three a.m. now, so it'll be soon. Won't be just you goin' alone boy. We all goin' together," Pop declared.

"I was so scared for all of us," Derrick sobbed.

"'Course you were, baby," Mom assured him, smoothing the damp hair back from Derrick's brow. "'Course you were. Seeing something so terrible as that . . . almost bein' shot. Anybody would go into a kind of shock. But now we gotta do the right thing."

Mom and Dad took their four other children to stay at their grandparents' house while they drove down to the police station. With his parents behind him, Derrick walked up to the front desk. "I want to talk to somebody who's working on the Wexford murder," Derrick announced in a shaky voice. "I was there. I saw the murder. I saw the whole thing go down."

The young sergeant looked up, startled. He glanced beyond the trembling teenager to his parents. "This is your son?" he asked.

"Yes," Derrick's father stated. "I am Guthrie Shaw and this is my wife, Florida. Our son is Derrick Shaw. He's a junior at Tubman High School. He's a very good boy, but he made a terrible mistake out of fear. He has come here to make that right, to tell you what happened. He's sorry he didn't come sooner, but the murderer threatened him and his family if he told. He was very much afraid and he still is, but he's goin' to tell you everything."

The sergeant asked Derrick and his parents to come to a room in the back. When they were seated, a thickset lieutenant entered the room and introduced himself. "I'm Lieutenant Hagbie, and I'm working on the murder investigation. Since the young man is a minor, you folks can sit in and listen to him give his statement." Derrick started to tell the police everything, from the moment he heard the shot in the alley until recently when he had encounters with B.J. and his girlfriend, Bethany Walsh.

"B.J.," Derrick related, "he said he had to kill me 'cause I was a witness, but I begged him for my life and he let me go. I promised him I'd never tell what I saw because I was so scared."

"What made you finally come in and talk to us, Derrick?" Hagbie asked.

"It was when you guys arrested Fabian. I couldn't keep quiet anymore," Derrick said. "I thought an innocent guy is gonna go to prison now 'cause I'm too much of a coward to talk."

Hagbie smiled thinly. "Rogers was released this morning," he told Derrick. "But I'm very glad you came in."

Derrick and his parents were shown a copy of Derrick's statement, and Derrick and his parents were asked to sign it.

"This is the beginning of a long process," Hagbie told them all. "We'll start looking for him right away and get him off the street as soon as we can. I have your contact information, and I'll keep you informed of any developments. Of course, B.J.'s threatened you, Derrick, and your family. So I'll put as much police surveillance as I can on your home, the middle school, and the high school. I can't guarantee twenty-four-seven coverage, but I'll have cars patrolling as often as I can. If you spot B.J. anywhere, call either the station or nine-one-one, and I'll have officers on the scene in minutes."

Derrick and his parents silently left the police station, somewhat comforted.

Pop had his arm around Derrick's shoulders. Mom said softly, "We love you baby. We're proud of you for doing the right thing today."

A terrible weight had been lifted from Derrick's shoulders, but the fear was more intense than ever. He had done what he swore he would never do—betray B.J. He dreaded the man's rage and vengeance.

When Derrick got to school, he did not tell anybody what he had told the police. He trusted only his closest friends. So he called Wes to say he couldn't come in that day and asked his friends to meet him after school at their hangout, the Coffee Camp. Trevor, Jaris, Alonee, and Sami were all there.

Derrick told his friends just what he had told the police in the morning.

"You saw the murder!" Alonee gasped. "Oh Derrick!"

"Keepin' quiet about it must have been eatin' you alive, child," Sami exclaimed. "How you been livin' with that?"

"I'm ashamed I didn't go to the police right away," Derrick moaned. "But I was so scared. I still am."

"I'd like to think I'd of gone right to the cops," Jaris said, "but to be honest, probably not. I mean, even getting past his threat to you, your family . . ."

"Even now," Derrick said, "if something were to happen . . . I mean, I couldn't live with it, if my sisters or brothers . . . Mom, Pop."

Jaris put his hand on Derrick's shoulder. "Gonna be okay man. The cops'll find him quick. He won't have a chance to do anything. He doesn't have a big operation around him. B.J.'s always been a loner criminal," Jaris assured him.

"Well, I did it. I came clean," Derrick declared. "I feel better about that. I don't feel good. I don't think I'll ever feel good about the thing, no matter what happens. It's a horrible picture in my mind, that dead guy. And I thought B.J. was going to kill me and he didn't, and that confuses me. What kind of a guy is he? I thought I knew him man. He was one of us, doing tricks on the skateboard. How . . . ?" Derrick raised his hands, palms upward, his head nodding left and right. He didn't have the answer to his own question.

Derrick had promised Destini he would take her to see a new group that mixed pop, new wave, and ska. He thought it would be good for him, too, to get his mind off what he had had to do. And he wanted the opportunity to tell Destini about everything, one on one. He didn't think she'd overreact, but, in case she did, at least he'd be able to talk with her without others around.

After the concert, Derrick told Destini everything he told his other friends and the police. He thought she had the right to know because he had put her in danger too. "So, if you don't want to hang with me for a while, Destini, I understand," he told her.

Destini put her arms around Derrick and gave him a long hug. "Oh wow! What a terrible thing you've been going through,

Derrick. And you had to keep it to yourself. That must have been awful. Oh baby, I'm so sorry you kept it all bottled up inside. It must have torn your heart to be covering up for that guy . . . but I understand. I can't imagine having to face such a choice ."

"Yeah, I wasn't sleeping or eating. I felt like a criminal myself," Derrick confessed.

"I wonder if they arrested B.J. yet?" Destini said. "And Bethany too. I bet they got them both."

"No," Derrick said. "This lieutenant at the police station, he said he'd call us if they catch him. And I know he'd do it 'cause he called my mom and told her they had the—what's it called?—warrant."

"Well, they're not saying much about it in the news. They're probably trying to sneak up on B.J.," Destini suggested. "If he doesn't know they know he did it, I bet B.J. won't even think you were the one who told the cops. I bet he won't even suspect you because you've kept quiet all this time. B.J. is gonna think the cops just put two and two together and came up with the truth."

"That'd be great," Derrick sighed, "but I'm not counting on that. I'm really looking around behind me all the time. I got this horrible feeling that somehow he knows what I did and—"

"It's scary," Destini interjected, putting her head on Derrick's shoulder. The park was emptying out, and the band was packing up its instruments. Twilight was settling in and the trees were laying down grotesque shadows. Suddenly, what was beautiful and dreamlike became threatening.

"I don't want to put you in danger, Destini," Derrick told her.

"You're not. I'm not afraid," Destini replied.

"If B.J. were out there shooting at me, you could get hit," Derrick said.

"He's not out there," Destini laughed. "I mean, he doesn't even know we're here.

It's not like our car is sittin' in the parking lot. We came by bus!"

"I know," Derrick said, putting his arm around the girl's soft shoulders. "But if something happened to you—"

"Oh Derrick, we take a chance every time we get up in the morning," Destini protested. "We could get struck by lightning, you know. Or maybe some space junk could fall from the sky and bop us on the head."

Derrick knew she was trying to make him feel better. But he didn't. "Come on, let's get out of here before it gets dark," he urged her, taking her hand.

CHAPTER EIGHT

Hi Derrick," Marko Lane called to Derrick on Monday morning. "What's goin' down?"

Derrick shrugged. "Huh?" he asked.

"I'm hearing a buzz that the cops are going to solve that college guy's murder," Marko responded. "My dad is real connected, and he's sayin' to me that they got their man. He's sayin' it maybe has something to do with you dude. So what's happenin'?"

"That's crazy," Derrick objected. "I don't know from nothin'."

Marko laughed. "Ain't that the truth though? You never do know what's happenin', man. But that's not what my father is hearing. There was an eyewitness to the murder. Man, whoever that dude was, it musta been some trip. It's one thing to see it happen in the movies, but to see it happening in real life, to see a guy getting offed . . . being right in the middle of it . . ."

Sami Archer was standing nearby. "Hey fool," she scolded Marko, "you makin' it sound like a wonderful thing to see a man cut down like that. Lissen up, sucka, if you was to see something like that, you'd wish you didn't. My daddy was in the war and he seen men cut in half with gunfire. He sometime wakes up in the middle of the night and he's sweatin' and cryin' 'cause he's livin' it all again 'cause you don't never get that out of your mind."

Derrick walked on to class. He hoped the whole mess would be over soon. He hoped the police would find and arrest B.J. Brady quickly. Derrick wasn't looking forward to the trial, to having to sit in that witness chair and look across the courtroom at B.J. But he would have to do it when the time came.

There was no turning back now. In fact, that morning Pop got a call from Lieutenant Hagbie. The police officer told him they were going to announce the warrant that afternoon.

At noon, the news broke. A police spokesperson appeared on a TV press conference to make the statement, and it was shown on the Tubman library set. A lot of students gathered to watch, including Derrick.

> After several weeks of investigation into the murder of Rafe Wexford, a graduate of Lincoln High School and a student at City College, we have identified a suspect. He is Bartlett Joseph Brady, age eighteen. Brady is described as five feet, six inches tall, about one hundred and forty pounds, dark-skinned, shaved head, dark brown eyes. He was last seen driving a red Maserati but probably has switched to another car. Brady is considered armed and dangerous. If anyone has any information on his whereabouts, please call the number now appearing on your screen.

Even though Derrick knew what was going to be said, the room started to swim around his head. All the faces of his fellow students blurred together. He felt as if he were underwater and drowning. There was a shark with terrible teeth closing on him.

B.J. was out there somewhere.

The spokesperson offered to answer a few questions and a reported asked, "Has a connection been established between the suspect and the dead man?"

"We are not commenting on the details of the case at this time," the officer answered.

"Are you pretty certain you've got the right guy?" another reporter asked. "A few days ago you grabbed a kid for the murder and that blew up."

"Based on our investigation, we are confident that Mr. Brady is the person we are looking for in this case," the officer stated.

A picture of B.J. Brady then appeared on the screen. It was a mug shot from one of his drug arrests. He had always beaten the rap in those cases.

"Oh man!" Marko Lane cried excitedly. "That little rat B.J. Brady did it. He murdered that guy! That little weasel used to go to school here. I always hated that little creep. I always knew he was a dirtbag. I remember him flying around the streets on his skateboard acting like he was king of the mountain. Man, I put him in his place. He thought he was such a hotshot on that board. I remember one time I seen him flying off his board and crashing. He skinned his knees, got all banged up. Looked like a fool lying there. I came along and I said, 'Hey runt, whatcha doing on the sidewalk? You're not so hot, are you midget?' "

Derrick and Jaris exchanged looks as Marko went on. "He was mad. He jumped up and came at me. No problem. I go, 'Hey midget, wanna fight? I can do that!' And I wrestled him down and pushed his dirty face in a fresh pile of manure they were spreading on the grass. Oh man, I bet he never forgot that!"

Jaris spoke up. "Marko, if I were you, I wouldn't be bragging about stuff like that. You and some other guys made B.J.'s life miserable. You picked on him because he was small. Maybe you guys played a part in turning him into what he is today."

"Ahhh, don't try to put it on me, Spain," Marko protested. "Everybody hated B.J. Even his parents couldn't stand him. One time I heard his old man saying to another guy that nobody else in the family was short like that, and why should his son be a 'dumb dwarf.' He was a dirty little freak. He always got what was coming to him. Too bad he didn't ride that skateboard in front of a garbage truck when he was a kid and get smashed before he had the chance to grow up."

Destini was standing next to Derrick as the police news conference ended. She linked her fingers with his, and they walked out together. "They'll get him," she whispered to Derrick.

"Yeah, but right now he's out there," Derrick said.

"The last thing he's thinking about is you, Derrick," Destini calmed him. "He just wants to get away. He knows he was eventually gonna be found out. Maybe he thinks that girl, Bethany, blew the whistle on him for all we know."

"He might escape into Mexico," Derrick suggested. "He was always clever. He got bad grades, but he was clever. He could hide out in some little fishing village in Mexico and then one day just pop back in town and find me."

"Derrick," Destini commanded, "don't torture yourself."

Derrick's father had told him last night that Derrick would not be riding his bike to the 99¢ store to work anymore. Pop planned to deliver Derrick and pick him up. When Derrick argued that this was too much trouble for his father, Pop glared at him and said, "You're my son, Derrick.

You're my firstborn. Ain't nothin' too much trouble in this whole entire world for me to do if it's keeping you safe. Y'hear what I'm saying boy?"

When Derrick's father arrived at Tubman, Derrick climbed into the old van with his father. "Did you hear the press conference from the cops, Pop?" Derrick asked.

"Sure did, son," Pop nodded yes. "They got their man identified, but he's on the run, looks like. What a terrible thing it all is. That little girl—Bethany Walsh. She was the nicest girl around our Talia. We felt so blessed to have her when we needed her. Well, you know what? Bethany's mother called us right after the press conference. She called us and she was all broken up."

"Has Bethany gone home?" Derrick asked.

"No, that's just the thing, Derrick," Pop replied. "They got no idea where their child is. They knew she was close to us, and they were hoping maybe she'd come to our house. Bethany hasn't been home in almost a year, ever since she got in with that bad crowd."

"Don't they have her phone number?" Derrick wondered.

"Her cell phone, yeah, but that's gone dead, her mom said. Poor mother has called all the kids Bethany used to know. Nothin'," Pop explained.

"I bet she went with B.J." Derrick knew he was right. "She's on the run with him. She told me she'd go wherever he went. She loves him so much."

"Ohhh," Pop groaned. "My heart just goes out to that poor family. They're good people, Derrick. They're really good people. How does something like this happen? They loved their children same as your mom and I do. I look at my kids—you, Bruce, Juno, the girls—and I would give my life for you kids. But I worry, Derrick. I worry about Bruce. Did you see how he was looking at B.J. going by in that Maserati, like the guy had it made? Easy money, the good life. Kids can get stupid and by the time they wise up, it's too late."

"Bruce is okay, Pop," Derrick assured him. "Don't worry about him. I'm takin' care of my brothers, Pop. I keep my eye on them."

When Derrick got to the 99¢ store, Wes was talking about the suspect in the Wexford murder. "So Derrick, the kid you were worried about is in the clear, eh? I told you they'd get the right one. This Brady guy, the one they're looking for. I've seen him on the streets dealing. He's bad news."

"Yeah," was all Derrick could say. He didn't want to share any information with Wes. The fewer the people who knew, the better. Derrick just wanted to concentrate on the good things happening now in his life—the better grades, this job he liked, Destini. Everything was getting better for Derrick. For a long time, a lot of kids were ragging on him for being stupid, but now things were looking up. Except for that horrible night in the alley . . .

It was almost eight at night when the phone rang at the 99¢ store. "For you, kid," Wes said.

Maybe Pop was going to be late picking him up. Derrick took the phone and said, "Yeah?" The phone went dead. Derrick thought the worst. B.J. was out there and he wanted to make sure Derrick was working tonight. Maybe he was across the street in the bushes with a high-powered rifle.

Derrick was shaking when he called home. "Mom, when Pop comes to pick me up, tell him to go around the back okay? Not the front like he usually does."

"Why? Is something wrong, Derrick?" Mom asked, her voice frightened.

"No, I don't think so. But I just got this phone call and when I answered, they hung up. Maybe just a wrong number, but I just want to be careful," Derrick answered.

"You think it might be B.J.?" Mom groaned.

"I'm just a nervous wreck, Mom. Just tell Pop to come around the alley," Derrick told her.

"Kid," Wes commented, "you're shaking like crazy. What's the matter? I heard you say you wanted to be picked up in the alley. What's going on?"

"I . . . I'm scared of that guy B.J.," Derrick blurted.

"*What*?" Wes demanded. "What have you got to do with him?"

"Wes," Derrick stammered. He didn't know how to tell him.

"Come out with it kid," Wes demanded. "You into drugs too. I thought you were clean. I never woulda hired you if I didn't think you were clean. You mixed up in that dirty drug business?" Wes sounded angry.

"I'm not into drugs, Wes. Never," Derrick told him. "But see, something happened that first night I started working here, when I was going home from work, from this job. I went through an alley and I saw B.J. kill that guy. B.J. said

140

he'd kill me if I didn't stay quiet about it, but I told the police and now I'm afraid he's after me."

Terror came to Wes's face. He was back in Basra. Men came in the night to kill anyone they had a grudge against. In those days, when he was Waleed, they came one night and killed Wes's brother-in-law in front of his wife and four children. Wes couldn't take any more violence. He grabbed his wallet and peeled off some bills. "This is what I owe you, kid," he spoke quickly and nervously. "And there's a little bit extra too. You're the best worker I ever had. But I want you to clear out of here tonight. And don't come back. I don't want somebody throwing a bomb through my window or shooting at the store with a rifle. I don't want some freaks blasting away at me or my family. I got a wife and kids. They need me. I'm sorry kid, just take the money. You're done here."

"I understand," Derrick said. "It's okay." He took the money and pushed it into his pocket. He loved this job. It was the best job he ever had. He liked Wes. But he understood. He went out the backdoor and waited in the alley for his father.

When the van pulled up, Pop shouted, "Everything okay?"

"Yeah," Derrick said, climbing in. "But Wes fired me. He just fired me."

"But you were doin' so good," Pop said.

"That phone call I got. It freaked me out, Pop," Derrick explained. "I started acting funny and Wes got wind of something wrong. I told him about me seeing B.J. that night in the alley and Wes went nuts. All the violence he saw back home in Iraq, it all came back to him. He didn't want a guy like me attracting trouble, you know. It's okay. I'm not mad at him or anything."

"Don't worry about it, Derrick," Pop soothed him. "I've been getting' more work. We'll do fine."

"Yeah, but I sure loved that job," Derrick said. "And that stupid phone call. Probably wasn't anything. But I can't help being afraid, Pop. I promised B.J. if he didn't shoot me I'd keep his secret. He's gotta know I ratted him out and he's gonna come after me. No matter what I did, you know, it was gonna be bad. I couldn't hide what he did forever, and still—I'm so scared now."

"Derrick, stop worryin' about it. Stop jumpin' at shadows, okay?" Pop insisted.

Derrick was exhausted when he got home. He tried to go right to bed and hoped he'd fall asleep, but he ended up like before, staring wide-eyed at the ceiling. It was like waiting for that other shoe to drop, waiting for B.J. to show up and take his revenge.

Suddenly Derrick heard yelling from the living room. "Derrick," Pop shouted, "it's all over the TV!"

Derrick jumped out of bed and ran to the living room. Even Bruce and Juno were out of bed and watching. The girls were supposed to be sleeping, but they showed up too. The television screen showed helicopters shining their beams on a twisting mountain road.

The news reporter was saying, "That's him in the black Ford pickup. The vehicle is owned by Bethany Walsh, B.J. Brady's companion. The police have been searching for the vehicle since they discovered it was missing."

The pursuit was taking place in the hilly country near the border between Mexico and the United States. There were police cars everywhere and they were chasing the black pickup.

"I guess he thought the Maserati was too easy to find," Bruce commented. "He musta ditched it."

Derrick stared at the TV screen. It was like watching a movie chase. But usually in the movies the villains were chasing the good guy. Here, the good guys were chasing B.J. The black pickup was careening around mountain road turns.

"Wow, look at them go!" Bruce exclaimed.

Derrick thought about Bethany Walsh, that poor girl in that pickup. She knew they couldn't escape, knew they were doomed. His heart ached for her. It was so sad that she decided to go with him to the bitter end.

Mom took the girls and Juno back to bed. She told them it was all over. Mom was afraid Talia would see something awful and later learn that Bethany Walsh was in that pickup truck.

When Mom returned, she remarked, "That poor child must be terrified."

Derrick recalled the times when Bethany babysat Talia. Bethany loved coins and she had a small collection. Derrick did too. Sometimes, when the family returned home, Bethany and he used to sit on the couch in the living room, comparing their coins. He could still hear Bethany giggling as they looked at the Susan B. Anthony coin, the gold Sacajawea, and the John F. Kennedy silver half-dollar. Bethany always joked about one day finding a really rare coin and being rich and famous.

"Ohhh!" Mom groaned. "That poor Walsh family must be watching this same as us. Can you imagine what they're going through?"

The TV reporter was doing a running commentary. "The highway gets extremely treacherous at this point. The police cars are slowing down, but the black pickup seems to be continuing at a reckless speed."

"Oh no!" Mom screamed. She covered her face with her hands. Then she moaned softly, "Oh no . . . oh no."

The pickup left the road. The television picture blurred. The black pickup that Derrick had sat in with Bethany that day seemed to be airborne. It was flying into a canyon hundreds of feet below.

"Bethany!" Mom cried.

The truck tumbled down the side of the canyon, pieces of it flying in all directions. It rolled to a stop, upside down, at the bottom. As the police helicopters got as close as possible and trained their spotlights on the wreck, a wisp of smoke went up from the engine. A minute or two passed, and a flame erupted on the ground under the vehicle. Getting to the site would take an hour or more, and everyone could only watch, knowing what would happen next. Then the fire flared up, fed by fuel on the ground, and the gas tank exploded. The truck disappeared in a huge ball of red-orange flame. A second later the sound of the explosion reached the news microphones and was broadcast to everyone watching at home. The truck was gone, and small fires burned in the grass and trees.

CHAPTER NINE

Derrick sat staring at the blank television screen long after Pop turned it off.

"It's so horrible, so horrible!" Derrick murmured, over and over. Tears ran down his face. He was stunned. For so long he had worried about B.J. tracking him down and taking vengeance. He saw B.J.'s face in every shadow, in every cluster of bushes or trees, in the darkness of every night. He went to bed at night haunted by the dead face of Rafe Wexford, and then terrified by the revenge he thought B.J. would wreak.

And now there was just emptiness. The fear was gone. But Derrick felt a terrible emptiness. The fear was dead. Bethany was dead. It didn't seem possible that all the guilt, all the fear, all the feverish terror could end in a burst of red-orange flame on the road to Mexico. It was almost as if this nightmarish ending would haunt Derrick as much as the night in the alley.

"Poor Mr. and Mrs. Walsh," Mom kept saying. "They lost their baby girl. I'd been talking to Bethany's mother. I kept telling her everything would be alright. I told her somehow her child would come home. It would be all right . . . and now . . . look . . ."

Nobody went to bed. They sat in the living room, talking about the old days that now seemed so far in the past that dinosaurs may as well have been roaming through their yards. They talked about when B.J. was a young boy and he'd come to play with Derrick. The boys would race around on their skateboards. Then they'd come inside, and Florida Shaw would give them homemade chocolate chip cookies and lemonade. B.J. talked about becoming a jet pilot. Sometimes he said he wanted to be a jockey because being small was a good thing for a jockey.

And they talked about Bethany's limitless patience with Talia, how she'd help Talia put up her dollhouse with all the tiny chairs and tables. Bethany would act out little dramas with the little people who lived in the doll-house. Nobody could make Talia laugh as Bethany could.

Derrick thought that it wasn't right. It wasn't fair. B.J. brought his destruction on himself, but it wasn't fair that he took Bethany with him. Her only crime was loving a very bad man, and she shouldn't have had to pay with her life.

The doorbell rang at three a.m. Every-body looked at one another. They thought perhaps the police had come to tell the Shaws that B.J. was dead and that Derrick needn't be afraid for his life anymore. But it wasn't the police.

Derrick's father looked out the peephole in the door before he opened it. He gasped. "Lord in heaven!" he cried, swinging open the door.

CHAPTER NINE

"Bethany!" Derrick's mother screamed. "Child, are you real, or are you a ghost?"

Bethany was sobbing and she said nothing. She was wearing only jeans and a tank top—no jacket or sweater—and was missing a shoe. Her hair was a tangled mess, with burrs from the bushes clinging to what once were curls. She had cried so much that her makeup was smeared all over her face. Her foot was bleeding, and she left red streaks on the Shaw carpet.

Derrick's mother put her arms around the girl and led her to the sofa. She sat her down, and Derrick brought a blanket to put around her shoulders. It was a cold night, and she was shivering. She had walked a mile or more from a nearby motel. She had seen what happened on television, and she began walking. She didn't know where to go. She couldn't go home—not looking like this and not when she didn't even know how her family felt about her anymore.

Bethany remembered the last place where she had been happy, before it all went wrong. It was at the Shaw house, taking care of Talia.

So that's where she went.

Derrick's father spoke softly into the phone in the corner of the living room. "Mrs. Walsh, lissen to me. Your daughter is alive. She wasn't in the pickup truck that crashed—what we saw on TV. She's here with us and *she's okay*. . . . . . . Yeah, I'm sure. She's been walking through the brush, but she's all right. . . . Lissen to me, Mrs. Walsh. We're helping her calm down. D'ya think you could give her a little while to get herself together? Maybe give us all here a few minutes for her to calm down? . . . Yes, I promise to call as soon as I can, probably only a few minutes. , , , Yes, she's okay. Just cold and scared, but she's all right. . . . You try to calm down yourself, Mrs. Walsh, and we'll call very soon. . . . Yes . . . You're welcome. . . . Good-bye for now." He put the phone down.

Derrick's mother brought a cup of hot cocoa with a marshmallow floating in it. In the winter, when Bethany babysat with Talia, she'd have a hot cocoa with a marshmallow with Talia before she went home.

Bethany sipped the cocoa slowly. The Shaws didn't ask her any questions, like why she wasn't in her black pickup with B.J. She was too fragile right now to talk. She seemed on the verge of a breakdown.

Then, after few minutes, Bethany began to talk.

"We hid out for a couple days, me and B.J., at the Stop Inn Motel, down the road" she started to explain. "We saw on TV that they knew he did it. So we hid out."

"Take it easy baby," Derrick's mother said soothingly. "Just take it easy."

"We packed to run off together," Bethany went on. "To Mexico. I loved him. He loved me."

Mom held the cup of cocoa for the girl to sip when her hand began to shake. "I told him I'd follow him anywhere. He said he knew that. He said nobody ever loved him like I did. That's what he said, over and over." Bethany's voice was a little stronger now. She finished the cocoa and closed her eyes. "I was so scared. I told him I didn't care what happens as long as we were together."

Pop brought a refill for the cocoa cup, and Mom held it again for Bethany. "You're doin' fine," Mom assured her.

"Last night we finished packing the truck. We were going to leave yesterday, but B.J. said we'd eat first. He got us some pizza and soda. B.J. kissed me and I kissed him. Then I felt so sleepy . . . last thing I remember B.J. was smiling at me and saying everything was cool. I didn't wake up till this morning. He was gone. He put sleeping pills in my soda. And he left me." She fumbled in her pocket for a scrap of paper. She handed it to Derrick's mother. "He left me this," Bethany explained, "with some money to pay the bill."

> Dear Bethany baby. Never forget that I loved you. Thanks for being the only one who ever loved me. Remember me. B.J.

"I guess he knew he didn't have a chance," Bethany said. "And he wanted me to have one. Even though I didn't want it without him."

"Baby," Mom said softly, "your mama's been crazy with worry. Your daddy too. They've been grieving for you for a good long time. They love you, child. Pop called them and told them you were okay and you were here. They want to come over to take you home."

"No!" Bethany cried, drawing her knees up under her chin. "No! I've done such horrible things. I'm not their daughter anymore. I've done drugs and sold drugs and hung out with terrible people. I don't want them to even look at me!"

"Baby, they love you with all their hearts," Mom pressed her. "Just now Pop talked to your mama and she was cryin'."

"I should have died with him in the truck!" Bethany sobbed. "They have to hate me for what I've done to them and I don't blame them."

"Baby girl," Mom insisted, "your mama and daddy want to come here and get their daughter. They don't hate you. They love you. For their sake, let them come. A long time from now, when you have a child of your own, you'll understand what they are feeling now. You cannot hate your child." Mom glanced over at her husband. She gave him a sign and he went into the other room to make the call.

In about five minutes, Derrick saw the headlights of a car shining through the front window of the Shaw apartment. Bethany's parents got out of the car. They were both crying. Mr. Walsh was a burly man with hands swollen and calloused from manual labor. The mother looked distraught.

The Shaws swung open their door and Bethany saw her parents. She pulled the blanket over her head and tried to hide. But her father came forward without a word and he picked the girl up in his arms as if she were not more than four or five. He held her and said, "Baby, baby, baby."

When she was a tiny girl he called her Beth-Boo. Now he whispered to her, "Praise the Lord you are home, Beth-Boo."

Bethany's mother kissed Bethany's cheek and told her, "Oh sweetheart, we love you so much."

"Thank you," the Walshes said to the Shaws as they hurried out with their sobbing daughter. Derrick couldn't hear anything Bethany said, just a stream of sobs. And then he heard her say just two words as the family vanished into the night. "Mommy . . . Daddy."

"What will happen to her?" Derrick wondered aloud.

"You told us she dealt crack," Pop said, "but the police probably don't have the goods on her. That fellow Wexford hadn't turned her in yet. So if her folks get her into rehab, she might be okay. She might have a chance."

Derrick thought about what B.J. had done. B.J. knew he couldn't escape but he tried. He must have thought he'd die in a hail of police bullets or in a prison cell. Whatever it would be, it would be ugly, and he didn't want Bethany to share that fate. So he drugged her and left her sleeping in her bed while he fled.

Derrick remembered something Bethany had said: "You don't understand B.J. I do. It takes somebody who loves him to understand. He's not all evil, Derrick."

The next afternoon, Derrick, Jaris, Trevor, Alonee, and Sami went down to the Coffee Camp. The old run-down hangout sold colas as well as lattes, and they all ordered sodas. They sat on the broken-down lawn chairs and logs to talk. The place was a hole in the wall right behind a thrift store and only the regulars knew it existed.

"I guess he had some good in him," Sami commented.

"My pop always says there's a little bit of good in the worst of us and a little bit of bad in the best of us," Jaris said. "I guess that's true."

"Pretty true," Alonee agreed.

"He spared my life that night in the alley," Derrick added. "He didn't have to do that. He coulda popped me off right then and there."

"Yeah, he did that," Sami said, "and he drugged Bethany to keep her from goin' down with him."

"I guess he knew it was hopeless," Trevor remarked. "B.J. was a small-time drug dealer and that was bad. But when he crossed over the line and killed that man, it had to have changed him. He knew he'd done something there was no coming back from."

"I wonder how B.J. would've turned out if all those kids hadn't bullied him," Jaris asked no one in particular. "Or if his parents had loved him even though he flunked school and was short and scrawny. I wonder if it would have all been different for him."

"Look at Derrick here," Sami pointed out. "How many times that creep of a

Marko makes fun of you? And me, I got a little too much weight on me, and you know how many times girls say ugly things to me and laugh behind my back?"

"Yeah," Derrick said, "but Sami, you and me, we got great parents."

"Yeah," Jaris agreed, "B.J. didn't have anybody. His father especially was disappointed in him and let him know it. B.J. was so cut off from his parents that when his mom died a couple months back, he didn't even know it until he read the obit in the paper."

"That's cold," Sami commented.

"Who knows about stuff," Trevor wondered. "Maybe we all got some monster hiding inside us waiting for the chance to come springing out."

Sami smiled. "We gotta make sure that old monster don't get the best of us, Trev. We owe it to each other. So you see some monster comin' along wantin' to get a hold of you, Trev, just holler and we'll all pounce on that sucka," she chuckled.

160

"So," Jaris announced, finally getting to the reason they had called this meeting. "There's gonna be a funeral, right?"

"They gotta bury him man," Sami asserted. "Least what's left of him. From the looks of the accident, he didn't leave much to bury. But I guess they put the remains in a box or something. Gotta do something. He got a father still livin'. Old man has to deal with it."

"So, we going or not?" Jaris asked at large.

"What do you say, Jaris?" Trevor replied. "The guy was a drug dealer and a murderer. He killed that war hero's son. Left a widow with no kids . . ."

"He was our pal, though, in the old days," Alonee remarked.

"He taught me how to skateboard," Derrick added. "I was no good at it, but he showed me the tricks."

"Me too," Jaris said. "He was the best skateboarder I ever saw. He fit in with us, 'cause we were younger and small like him."

"So Derrick, it's your call," Trevor put it to him.

"Why's it my call?" Derrick asked.

"'Cause man, you got the biggest stake in this," Trevor said. "Look at all the misery B.J. caused you after you witnessed the murder. But he spared your life. He did that. But he messed up your life too. If you say we shouldn't go, Derrick, then we won't go. Does everybody agree?"

Alonee, Sami, and Jaris nodded.

"Sounds fair to me," Sami said.

Derrick finished his soda. He remembered the last time he saw B.J. It was when B.J. gave him that hundred dollars, along with the veiled threats. Derrick had never been as afraid of anybody as he was of B.J. Derrick figured that as long as he lived he would remember that night in the alley and his terror facing B.J.'s gun.

And yet B.J. was a person. He was a human being. Derrick couldn't hate anybody. It just wasn't in him to hate anybody. "I say go," he said softly. "I say we go to the funeral. He was, you know, a homie. He was . . . *one of us*."

The next day, Derrick's father received a phone call from Wes. Derrick was more than welcome to return to his own job, with a little extra in his pay too. Wes had heard about B.J. taking the fatal dive off the canyon. He saw no reason not to take back the best employee he ever had. When Derrick dropped by the store, Wes said, "I hope there are no hard feelings, kid."

"No, Wes. I understood," Derrick assured him.

"I rejoice in no man's death," Wes went on, "but I guess it's best what happened."

"I'll start work again on Monday," Derrick said. "I got to go to a funeral Saturday or I'd start then."

"My condolences, kid. I hope it was nobody close," Wes said.

"Thank you," Derrick replied.

Derrick climbed back on his bicycle and headed home. It had been some time since he rode his bicycle like this, never looking behind him in fear. He looked at the old familiar sights he always enjoyed passing—the house with the black lab dogs, the store that never took down its Christmas decorations. Derrick often whistled as he biked. He wasn't quite ready to whistle yet. He had been afraid for a long time.

Derrick thought it would never be quite the same again. When big things like this happen, they change a person. Life is never exactly the same. For example, Derrick would never ride his bike down that alley again. Nor would he ever go there driving or walking or in any way, shape, or form.

Derrick had not been to too many funerals in his life. Once, a long time ago, he attended his grandfather's funeral. The man had had a good, long life and it was not a particularly sad occasion, especially since the singing was joyful and rousing. It was almost like a merry band was accompanying Grandpa to a happier place. Derrick was ten at the time and he wasn't terribly sad at all.

But Derrick was feeling very strange about B.J.'s funeral. For one thing, B.J. was too young to die, but then so was Rafe Wexford. It was just a terrible tragedy all around. But Derrick had never met Rafe Wexford in life, and he had known B.J. from childhood.

It seemed that one minute B.J. was teaching Derrick how to do tricks on the skateboard, and the next minute he was holding that gun and threatening to kill him.

Derrick was told that he needed a good, dark suit for the funeral. He usually wore T-shirts and jeans in the summer, and jeans and a jacket in the winter. So he had no good dark suit. His father had one, but they were not the same size. Derrick finally borrowed a dark suit from Trevor's brother, Tommy. It did not fit exactly right but it was the best he could do.

CHAPTER TEN

Most of the people in the neighborhood around Tubman High School considered B.J. Brady a very low form of life. The kids at Tubman didn't know him well, and those who knew him by his reputation feared and disliked him. And, in fact, he was a criminal and a murderer. He was a stunning example of failure in the neighborhood. He was the poster boy for what went wrong in families losing their children to drugs or gang violence. So hardly anybody wanted to come to his funeral. In fact, many felt it was a disgrace even to have a funeral for him.

However, when Mr. Brady, the father, came to see Pastor Bromley about services, the pastor was his usual compassionate self. He assured the father that no one was beyond the mercy of God and, of course, he would conduct services for his son. Mr. Brady was a respectable man who had owned a furniture store in the neighborhood for many years and he was bitterly ashamed of B.J. Still, he wanted a funeral for his son if for no other reason than his neighbors and business associates would think it was shocking that a father would not want to have a decent funeral for his child.

None of the teachers at Tubman High— even those who remembered B.J. Brady as a student in their classes—wanted to attend the funeral, except for one. Ms. McDowell announced to her classes that she would be attending the funeral and that she had a van that would seat as many as eight students if anybody wanted to come. A few of the other teachers disapproved of her announcement and even some parents were shocked.

Derrick, Jaris, Trevor, Destini, Alonee, and Sami all accepted Ms. McDowell's invitation to ride to the funeral with her. Nobody else did.

"You guys must be crazy," Marko Lane laughed after American history class. "You going to the funeral of a dirty drug dealer who killed a guy? What's that all about? He shouldn't even have a funeral. They should take his ashes out to the city dump and put them there 'cause he was nothin' but trash."

"B.J. had a father," Jaris told Marko. "This guy is coming to church to attend his son's services. He's a father. You want him to be all alone in the church?"

"Like I care!" Marko said. "The old dude should be ashamed to show his face in public anyway. He raised a cold-blooded killer. What's he want to make a show of it now anyway?"

"Maybe he didn't start out to raise a bad guy, fool," Sami chimed in. "Maybe he tried his best and it just didn't work out. The world's full of criminals and it ain't all the parents fault. People got choices. Sometime they make bad choices. Or even

if the father did bad when he raised B.J.,
even then we got to show some respect for
the man's grief."

"We're goin' to the funeral because he
was one of us," Derrick stated. "He was
born in the same hospital we were born
in. He played with us on these sidewalks.
Once he was a kid here at Tubman. He
was one of us."

" 'One of us'," Marko snarled. "Maybe
one of you guys, your little group of stupid
idiots, but he was never part of anything I
belonged to. They ought to erase his name
from the records here at the school. They
ought to deny that the creep ever existed.
And I don't think much of Ms. McDowell
either, going to the funeral, driving kids
there. But I guess she's got a sleazy brother,
so maybe she feels close to losers like that."

"Shane Burgess is doing great in his
school," Alonee asserted. Ms. McDowell's
younger brother had been in some trouble
with gangs, and the teacher took the boy
under her wing. Now he went to a special

school and was in rehab, and he hoped to return to Tubman soon.

"The poor kid had no family and he got mixed up in bad stuff," Trevor said. "He's not sleazy. Since Ms. McDowell has been looking after him, he's okay. You make me sick, Marko. You got no heart."

"You got no brains, Trevor," Marko snapped. "You and that idiot Derrick. All you goofy fools. I'd be ashamed to walk into that church and show everybody that I thought B.J. Brady was somebody who deserved to be mourned."

Sami laughed loudly. "Marko Lane, good thing you ain't goin' in that church, 'cause the walls could just fall down on you. You think you so high and mighty, but you got no pity for anybody. Never did."

"You have no empathy," Alonee added.

"Empathy?" Marko sneered. "That sounds like a disease. What's empathy?"

"Empathy, that's like having sympathy for other people," Alonee explained. "Not having sympathy, *that's* the disease."

"Yeah, sucka," Sami joined in. "If you had had some kindness toward that B.J. when he was still a little kid, maybe he woulda turned out better."

"Listen to the fat girl," Marko sneered. "If she had as many brains as she's got pounds, she'd be the smartest chick at Tubman."

"Marko Lane, you the stupidest dude ever went to this school," Sami told Marko off. "Sometimes I feel like goin' up to the statue of Harriet Tubman and putting a blindfold over her eyes when you come sashayin' in 'cause she too fine a lady to have to look at you."

Saturday morning—the day of the funeral—dawned cloudy and cold. The weatherman was predicting rain. It matched the mood of the six students who met in the Tubman High parking lot and climbed into Ms. McDowell's van.

Ms. McDowell started talking as soon as the van was in motion. "You guys, I was in trouble when I was a kid in a neighborhood just like this one. We had drugs and gangs and a lot of kids going over the edge. I was one of them. One day I went to the library and I checked out a book by John Steinbeck—*The Grapes of Wrath*. An elderly lady noticed I had the book and we started talking. Pretty soon I was pouring out my heart to this lady. She turned out to be one of those angels who really wanted to help kids at risk. Anyway, she became my friend, my mother, I guess, because my own mother was dead. Because of her I started college and got into teaching. I'm telling you guys this because it just proves how much difference one good person can make."

"Is this lady still living?" Derrick asked.

"No," Ms. McDowell responded, "she was alive all during my college years and she saw me graduate and get my first teaching job. She shared in all the exciting days when I was starting out. My parents were dead, my brothers and sisters were all scattered. She was my family when I really needed one. Adelaine Baxter. When she died, I cried for her like you would for a mom. Do you see how sometimes one person can make all the difference and how you can be that one person for someone?" The question hung in the air for a second.

"Yeah," Jaris answered, "I guess B.J. didn't have that one person."

"No special angel," Alonee said.

"Sometimes you don't even know that somebody need a special angel," Sami added. "We all so busy just doin' our own thing, we never see the person hurtin' there in the corner."

"Just try," Ms. McDowell urged. "I think being here today says something about all of you. And who knows what special need there is for us to be here today. Who knows?"

When they got into the church, hardly anyone was there. Bethany and her parents sat way over to the side. There were some strange-looking young men dressed in gang clothing, probably associates of B.J. during his various activities. And in the front row sat a man in a business suit, about forty-five years old.

"That's Elwood Brady," Alonee whispered. "B.J.'s father. We went in his store a few times."

Derrick looked at the man. He kept checking his watch, as if he didn't want to be here and hoped it would be over soon. He didn't look left or right. If he had noticed that the church was almost empty, he showed no sign. He sat there stiffly, as if there were an invisible wall around him and he preferred that nobody bridged it to speak to him. However, Pastor Bromley came over to offer his condolence and shake hands, as he did with all relatives of the deceased. Elwood Brady shook hands as briefly as he could. Pastor Bromley glanced around the church then, sadly noting the emptiness. It was painfully clear that few mourned the passing of B.J. Brady.

There was no coffin, of course, but there was a small wooden box sitting on a little walnut table. Two vases, each containing a single red rose, stood watch over the box. Derrick figured all B.J.'s earthly remains were in that wooden box.

Pastor Bromley was mercifully brief in his remarks. He read from scripture and referred to the mercy of God for all sinners. A slender old lady sat at the piano and accompanied herself singing "Amazing Grace." And then it was over.

Derrick didn't know if he should say something to Mr. Brady. The young men, who probably were B.J.'s criminal accomplices, left the church quickly and in a defiant way. Derrick hoped that none of them had been tipped off that he had betrayed B.J. He thought not because none of them cast a look in his direction.

Bethany walked up to the wooden box, leaned over, and kissed it. She burst into tears then and rushed into her parents' arms. They all walked out of the church slowly and somberly. Nobody was saying anything to Mr. Brady, who seemed a pathetic figure sitting there alone in the front pew. Derrick thought he probably should try to say something, even though he didn't want to. Derrick made his way to the front of the church and stopped at the man's pew.

"I'm real sorry, Mr. Brady," Derrick said to him.

"Are you one of his low-life friends who helped drag him down into the pit of destruction?" Mr. Brady snarled. His eyes were black with rage.

"No sir," Derrick responded in his usual friendly way. "I was friends with him when we were kids and we played together and he went to Tubman when I did. I just wanted to tell you I'm sorry you lost your son."

Mr. Brady glared at Derrick as if he didn't believe him. The man's face was fixed and cold. He looked like he hadn't had a kind thought in years. "I lost my son a long time ago. As far as I'm concerned he's been dead for years. Buried in cocaine." With that, the man stood and moved toward the door.

"Mr. Brady!" Pastor Bromley called out. He was holding the wooden box containing B.J.'s ashes. "The remains, Mr. Brady." He held the box toward the father.

"Do whatever you want with it," Mr. Brady snapped, hardly breaking his stride toward the door.

"But Mr. Brady," Pastor Bromley said in a helpless, pleading voice. The minister looked at the box forlornly when the father was gone, as you might look at an abandoned baby.

"We'll take it," Ms. McDowell offered. She reached out for the box with her beautiful hands.

The six students and Ms. McDowell walked out of the church toward the parking lot. Ms. McDowell handed the box to Derrick. He held it nervously. It was a pretty walnut wood box with a crucifix carved on the top of it.

"Look," Jaris pointed, "Bethany and her parents are still here."

Ms. McDowell walked over to the Walshes and they talked for several seconds. Then Ms. McDowell turned and called out to Derrick, "Bring the box."

Derrick handed the box to Bethany. She was still crying. She got into the family car, holding the box tightly. And then they drove away.

"That was the right thing to do," Derrick told his teacher.

"Yes," Ms. McDowell agreed, "Nobody else wanted him, even in death. You see, you guys? That's why we came today. That was our purpose, though we didn't know it."

Ms. McDowell offered to take everybody home. Derrick put his arm around Destini's shoulders as they rode away from the church. Ms. McDowell dropped Jaris and Trevor, and Sami and Alonee off. Then she dropped Derrick and Destini at Destini's mother's duplex.

"I want you to meet my mom," Destini said as they walked together toward the apartment. "I told her about you and she's been real anxious to meet you. She said she'd make us a nice meal."

"I gotta tell Mom," Derrick said. Destini gave him her cell phone, and he told his mother he was eating over at Destini's house and he'd be home later.

Derrick didn't expect this. He knew he liked Destini and she liked him, but dinner at her mom's place? Derrick was a little nervous. He wasn't very good at charming people, especially older people, like past thirty-five. Most people who first met Derrick thought him awkward and stupid. It didn't help that he was wearing Tommy Jenkins's suit, which was a size too big.

"Mom!" Destini called out when they got inside. "This is my boyfriend, Derrick."

Destini's mother looked Derrick over. She wasn't too thrilled about Destini having another boyfriend. The last one was a disaster. He battered Destini. But this boy looked different. He was cute, but not handsome. He looked as though he'd just been shucking corn and had fallen off a turnip truck or something.

"Hello Derrick," Destini's mother finally said. "I made meatloaf and gravy and mashed potatoes and apple pie."

"I like plain food," Derrick said. "My mom makes good stuff like that."

Destini's mother grinned. She liked the boy.

As they ate, Destini's mother commented, "My, you are a nice looking boy in a suit and all. Don't see many boys your age wearing suits when they step out on a date."

"I don't usually wear suits," Derrick admitted. "This isn't even mine. I borrowed it. I just came from a funeral." Destini was giggling. She covered her mouth. Derrick continued, "I got no funeral-going suit of my own."

Destini's mother laughed too, but not in a mocking way. "Child," she said, "I think you picked well this time. I like this boy just fine."